Second Chances

PEGGY CHERNOW

Copyright © 2020 Peggy Chernow.

All rights reserved. No part of this book may be reproduced, stored, or transmitted by any means—whether auditory, graphic, mechanical, or electronic—without written permission of the author, except in the case of brief excerpts used in critical articles and reviews. Unauthorized reproduction of any part of this work is illegal and is punishable by law.

This is a work of fiction. All of the characters, names, incidents, organizations, and dialogue in this novel are either the products of the author's imagination or are used fictitiously.

ISBN: 978-1-71694-345-4 (sc)
ISBN: 978-1-71694-346-1 (hc)
ISBN: 978-1-71694-344-7 (e)

Library of Congress Control Number: 2020907330

Because of the dynamic nature of the Internet, any web addresses or links contained in this book may have changed since publication and may no longer be valid. The views expressed in this work are solely those of the author and do not necessarily reflect the views of the publisher, and the publisher hereby disclaims any responsibility for them.

Any people depicted in stock imagery provided by Getty Images are models, and such images are being used for illustrative purposes only.
Certain stock imagery © Getty Images.

Lulu Publishing Services rev. date: 04/29/2020

To my special friends and family (they know who they are), who have helped me in so many ways during the process of writing this book, but especially Shandee, Brenda, and Robbie. Their technical expertise and computer knowledge have been invaluable. The manuscript would never have made it to the publisher without them. And as always, this book is dedicated to my greatest fan and biggest supporter, my wonderful husband, Bart.

Sometimes goodbye is a second chance.

—Shinedown

PROLOGUE

Darcy and Danielle clutched each other's hand in mutual anguish. Experiencing unimaginable sorrow, they stood stoically and watched in disbelief as the shiny mahogany casket was lowered silently into the ground. Neither twin could allow her eyes to look anywhere else. Holding each other's hand, they fought gallantly to control their emotions and endure the heart-wrenching moment. Their sadness was so profound, their emotions so raw, that they couldn't begin to acknowledge the well-meaning condolences from the dozens of prominent mourners who had traveled from all around the country to attend the burial service.

Part 1

CHAPTER 1

Danielle

Danielle sat at her kitchen table, sipping hot water with lemon and nibbling on a dry saltine. Two-year-old Freddy, named after Danielle's deceased father, Fred Coulter, played happily nearby with the newest toy from his aunt Darcy and uncle Mark. Danielle took deep breaths and fought the familiar waves of nausea as she tried to focus on the exciting morning's headline from the *New York Times*. NATHAN PIERCE, JUNIOR SENATOR FROM MASSACHUSETTS, EXPECTED TO WIN THE PRESIDENCY IN LANDSLIDE TONIGHT. Danielle smiled despite her physical discomfort. It was such wonderful news.

Alex, dressed in an immaculate gray suit with a maroon-striped tie, strolled casually into the room and kissed his wife affectionately on her cheek. "Are you feeling any better this morning, honey?" he asked with concern. He thought she looked a little green.

This second pregnancy wasn't going as smoothly as her first. Little Freddy had been a breeze, delivered on time and with little trauma. On the other hand, Baby Caroline, as Danielle and Alex had decided to name their firstborn daughter, had been a bit more demanding and problematic. Even in her sixth month, Danielle was still experiencing debilitating morning sickness, and the baby kicked so often and hard at night that Danielle had difficulty sleeping. Sometimes she was so exhausted that she wasn't sure she could last until her due date in mid-February.

Alex felt empathy for his wife, and as much as he adored her, there was nothing he could do to help. He was a wonderful, caring husband and a great father to Freddy. When his busy schedule at the hospital allowed, he took the adorable toddler on outings to the zoo, the park, and, the biggest treat of all, upstairs to play with Danielle's twin sister, Darcy, and her husband, Mark, in their apartment. These little excursions gave Danielle some much-appreciated time to nap.

"I'm okay," she answered, gingerly taking another bite of the cracker. "Take a look at the paper." Danielle handed Alex the *Times*. "It all but declares that Nathan will win the presidency tonight. I'll call Connie when my stomach settles down to congratulate her. She must be so excited and very frightened at the same time. It's an awesome task she and Nathan are about to assume.

"Remember when she became First Lady of Massachusetts? She was so worried about doing and saying the right thing; and she wanted so much to be an asset, a real political partner to Nathan. How times have changed. Now she's as popular in the polls as he is, maybe more so, and she does almost as many interviews and guest appearances on television. She'll make a fabulous First Lady for the country. I'm so proud of them both and happy that they're our friends."

"Me too," he replied enthusiastically. "It's hard to remember a time when Connie and Nathan weren't in our lives in some way. It seems like ages ago when their only son, Frank, was brought into the emergency room at Massachusetts General Hospital and my surgical team and I worked around the clock to save him. That Thanksgiving night changed all our lives forever."

"Yes, it did," Danielle agreed. "I remember everything about Frank's long, painful recovery, and that's when our friendship with Connie and Nathan began. It's amazing to realize that the sixteen-year-old mischievous boy we cared for then is now all grown up with a wife of his own."

"Honey." Alex changed the subject. "A word of advice. I'd be a little cautious offering the Pierces premature congratulations. Remember, not too long ago, all the polls had forecast Hillary Clinton winning, and then at the last minute Donald Trump swooped in and claimed the victory. I doubt anything like that would ever happen again, but just in case, I don't think we should celebrate before the final results are known. There'll be time enough for that at tonight's election party after all the votes have been counted. For now, just call Connie and wish them good luck from both of us."

"I suppose you're right," Danielle reluctantly agreed. "I pray for the country's sake that Nathan *does* win. We need him to turn things around."

"You're preaching to the choir." Alex smiled. He knew Danielle was passionate about her politics, as was he. "I've got to get to the hospital now. Lots of meetings and some problems with scheduling for the third-year residents. But don't worry. I'll be home in plenty of time to take you to the festivities tonight. Do we have our regular babysitter for Freddy?"

"Yes, of course. She'll be here by seven. Darcy and Mark will be coming with us." Danielle stood up and hugged him. "Have a good day. I love you, Dr. Alex Stone."

"I love you too, Dr. Danielle Stone." He picked up his son and kissed Freddy on the top of his curly, red hair. "You look so much like your grandfather," he said nostalgically. "If he were alive today, he'd adore you. Our little carrottop."

Danielle smiled warmly at the memory of her father, who had passed away several years earlier. Theirs hadn't been an easy father-daughter relationship, but at the end of his life, all splintered fences had been mended and years of misunderstandings settled and forgiven. Fred had died as a happy man, surrounded by his two identical twin daughters and the men they loved.

Danielle glanced over at the staircase leading up to the second floor of their duplex. Under it stood a life-size, metal statue of a physician, which Danielle had bought from a funky Greenwich Village shop shortly after they moved from Boston to New York City. She and Alex had named him "Hippocrates" after the father of medicine. The statue had become an integral part of their family and was an ongoing private joke between them. Alex fist-bumped the statue's hand. "Take care of Mommy and Freddy for me today," he instructed Hippocrates as he headed out the door.

Suddenly, Danielle bolted for the bathroom. Baby Caroline was making her presence known once again.

CHAPTER 2

Darcy

Darcy and Mark left the grueling four-hour production meeting for next week's *Speaking of Sports with Donavan & Donavan* shows. It was early November, so most of the upcoming television segments would concentrate on the National Football League games, and a few would cover the approaching college basketball season. Darcy took the tapes from her husband, Mark Donavan, and shoved them and other paperwork into her black crocodile briefcase. She would try to study them when she got home, unless she could come up with a plausible excuse not to. Mark, as usual, was staying at the studio a little later to rehearse and tape a piece for the evening local and national news. He put in much longer hours than Darcy but didn't seem to mind. He loved his job. He and Darcy had no children, so their sports show was his "baby."

Darcy and Mark had been coanchoring their highly acclaimed sports talk show, which had been a top money-making program on ESPN, for the last five years. They constantly traveled around the country, bringing their own brand of humor and vast sports knowledge to local and national audiences. They covered the NFL, NBA, major league baseball, and college sports of all kinds. Some less-than-ethical team owners and selfish players tried to exert pressure on them to slant their coverage in a certain direction from time to time. But Mark and Darcy were scrupulously honest and steadfastly rejected the improper overtures.

Wherever there was an important sports event, the two were there, microphones and cameras ready. They were wildly popular as a couple and often drew large crowds of spectators, who wanted to get a personal glimpse of the famous married couple at work. They were extremely gracious to their fans and at Mark's insistence often stayed around after the games to take selfies and pose for pictures with the crowd. He used to joke that he'd never met a flashbulb or a camera he didn't like.

When Mark first suggested to Darcy that she coanchor a sports talk show with him, she had been apprehensive but ecstatic. She had no television experience but a vast knowledge and love of all sports. Originally, she found broadcasting to be exciting and challenging, and she could hardly wait to get to work each day. She loved the opportunity to bring interesting and quirky sports stories to life for the general public. Most of all, she loved working with her husband, Mark. *Speaking of Sports with Donavan & Donavan* had been a dream come true for them both.

But now, after over five years of filming hundreds and hundreds of shows, her enthusiasm had greatly diminished. She felt that every football and baseball stadium had begun to look and smell alike. The grimy press boxes in every venue appeared to be almost identical, even down to the discarded, cheese-stained pizza boxes and half-full soda cans strewn haphazardly about. The overcooked hot dogs and stale beer tasted in Detroit or Denver like they did in Atlanta or Miami. The raucous, screaming fans, dressed in their team's vibrant-colored jerseys, and the perky cheerleader's skimpy outfits all faded into one blurred and monotonous montage.

The thrill of victory and the agony of defeat were no longer earth-shatteringly important to her. Her attitude about sports and its importance had gradually changed. The outcome of a particular game wasn't as crucial or significant anymore, with the exception of the Washington Redskins football games. Often after working a game or conducting an interview, she felt oddly depressed. *There has to be something else. Something more meaningful that I can do with my life*, she thought but never dared verbalize to her husband.

She desperately wanted to share her unsettling feelings with Mark but dreaded his reaction. She knew him so well. Sports had always been his life's work, and he never seemed to tire of any aspect of it. To the contrary, being a commentator was all he had ever wanted to do. And now he was at the top of his profession, the most sought-after sportscaster in the nation. How could she simply ask him to walk away from that? Could she on a whim willingly break up such a successful broadcasting partnership and risk hurting her marriage?

Mark would feel shocked, heartbroken, and betrayed when he learned how she felt now about their show and careers. In the beginning, the talk show had been their shared perfect dream, but over time it had become a nightmare for Darcy.

As each day passed, she became more listless and unhappy. She hid her emotions well, but the stress was causing her to have stomach problems, headaches, and sleepless nights. She was losing weight. Mark accused her of taking the Weight Watchers diet too far. She secretly yearned to become just a fan again and simply watch a game for pleasure instead of having to analyze it from every angle for their radio or televisions audiences.

Darcy, who had lived and breathed sports since she was a child and had been (and still was) a lifelong Redskins football fan, understood she was at a personal crossroads. She was thirty-six years old and believed she was destined to undertake something more challenging and useful with her life with the more than $40 million she'd inherited from her father. She knew it was time for something different. She had to make a change …

She loved and respected her twin sister, Danielle, who had given up her career as a dermatologist to develop a program to help cancer patients cope with the difficult disease and its lifestyle ramifications. Over time, Danielle had started an innovative creative writing program for patients undergoing chemotherapy and called it Healing Words. Now, because of Danielle's hard work and a sizable inheritance from their father, that program had grown immensely popular and spread from hospital to hospital. It helped thousands of suffering patients every day. Darcy appreciated and admired what Danielle had accomplished, and she wanted to find something as fulfilling for herself and Mark.

But what?

Darcy also adored and admired her brother-in-law, Alex Stone, a talented trauma surgeon. As a result of a freak accident several years ago, in which he had broken his right hand, he had been unable to continue operating. Instead of giving in to self-pity and depression, he had rethought his career goals, moved from Boston to New York City, and accepted a nonoperating position at a prestigious hospital there. He became the vice chair of the Surgical Education Department and was responsible for the curriculum of all medical students, interns, and residents.

Since making that daunting career change, he had become the recipient of numerous teaching awards and was beloved and revered by his students and the hospital staff. He thrived on teaching and mentoring the medical students and found these pursuits immensely rewarding. Darcy was secretly envious of the happiness Alex's new career had given him. She wanted to feel that proud of her own job. She just didn't.

She couldn't help but contrast what she and Mark did professionally (jetting off to NCAA tournaments and Super Bowls, and chatting endlessly on air about sports minutia) with Danielle and Alex's career choices. Darcy's work seemed so superficial and shallow in comparison. At the end of the day, she could dust her many broadcasting awards, but they gave her no pleasure, no real sense of satisfaction. She thought her television show, *Speaking of Sports with Donavan & Donavan*, though hugely successful and an impressive source of income for the network, was tiresome and unimportant. No matter what the personal consequences, she had to make Mark understand how empty and ungrounded she felt. How could she make him realize that they needed to do something more lasting and worthwhile with their time and talents?

She dreaded having this conversation with Mark. He would think she had lost her mind and was being ungrateful and childish. What woman wouldn't want to be the star of her own television show? Be wined and dined all over the country by appreciative television executives and advertisers? And be swarmed by adoring fans? Mark loved the attention his celebrity brought, but Darcy was tiring of it and felt less comfortable in the spotlight. She had to make her husband understand … and soon. She wasn't sure how long she could keep up the charade.

CHAPTER 3

Danielle and Darcy

Danielle and Alex walked into Senator Nathan Pierce's election headquarters on Madison Avenue. Darcy and Mark followed closely behind them. The two twins always drew special attention. Everyone seemed fascinated by how much they looked alike, and people couldn't keep themselves from staring at the sisters. Darcy and Danielle had experienced that reaction their whole lives, so they didn't even appear to notice nowadays.

A large, jubilant crowd had gathered, celebratory drinks in hand, around dozens of TV screens and were watching the national broadcasters tally the voting results. The Deep South and early results from the East Coast revealed a trend, predicting a possible landslide for the charismatic young senator from Massachusetts. The polls were still open in the West. CNN, Bloomberg, and CNBC held out a slim hope that the former speaker of the house, Bill Mitchell, would eventually prevail. But FOX, ABC, NBC and CBS were certain Senator Nathan Pierce would be the next president of the United States. However, they were reluctant to make the official announcement until all the polls, including those in Hawaii, had closed.

"I can't stand this," Danielle shouted over the noise of the crowd. "I'm so nervous and excited. I never really believed this election would actually happen." She reached for a glass of mineral water from a waitress's tray.

"I'd love a glass of champagne," she complained to her sister. "But I'll have to wait until our little miss Caroline makes her appearance."

"I know," Darcy answered in sympathy as she reached for a flute of the bubbly. "Just a few more months. The time will go quickly. I can't wait to meet my little niece. And by then, hopefully Nathan will have been sworn in as president."

"Hold your horses," Alex warned the sisters. "Remember what they say. 'It's not over till the fat lady sings.'"

"Don't be such a pessimist." Mark laughed. "We're not dealing with voter fraud or hanging chads now. This has been an open and honest election … fair and balanced, as a certain network has claimed."

"Is there really any such thing?" Alex persisted. "That would mean we have ethical politicians and unbiased reporters. I honestly don't think that's the case anymore."

"Well, we certainly have an honest guy in Nathan," Danielle insisted. "You'll never meet a more upstanding, principled guy."

"I agree with that," Alex said. "I was speaking about politicians in general, certainly not about Nathan. Why don't we try to find a table where we can put our drinks down and watch the televisions? I think Danielle should get off her feet."

Darcy looked around the room at all the smiling, happy faces. They were exuberant and could taste victory. The atmosphere was electric. This time the polls had been correct. Nathan was going to win. She pointed at an empty table at the back of the room and started to make her way there. Several Pierce supporters recognized Mark and Darcy, and approached them for autographs and pictures. Mark and Darcy were gracious as usual and signed their names on several "Pierce for President" cocktail napkins; they also posed for pictures with campaign workers. After exchanging pleasantries with the fans, Darcy grabbed Mark's hand and moved to the table to join Danielle and Alex.

"From the minute I met Connie and Nathan, I knew they were destined for great things. Ginger must be in seventh heaven now," Darcy said with affection. "And now that Ginger's younger brother is about to become the president of the Unites States, her status as the grand dame of Washington Society will be assured for the next four and maybe eight years."

"By the way, how is our friend, Ginger?" Danielle asked. Since Freddy's birth and now that he was in "the terrible twos," she had been too busy between her work for Healing Words and motherhood to keep up with Darcy's former cast of characters from her previous life in Washington. "Is she still so formidable?"

"Yes, of course," Darcy answered warmly. Ginger was like a second mother to her. They had quite a long and complicated history together and shared a deep affection for each other. Several years ago, Ginger had graciously thrown a beautiful wedding reception after Darcy and Mark married in New York. It was held several months later at the prestigious Chevy Chase Club in suburban Maryland and had been considered the social event of that season. "She calls me at least once a week and fills me in on all the DC gossip. She loves hearing my TV scuttlebutt. I wish I could see her more often. Sometimes I wish we still lived in DC. It was so exciting and enjoyable there ... less hectic."

"I bet we'll all see a lot more of her now that Connie and Nathan will be living in the White House." Danielle grinned. "I'm sure she'll find a way to host a lot of functions there and place herself front and center. She was never shy."

"You know her too well." Darcy laughed. "She'll be in her element." Just the mention of Ginger and DC stirred up memories and made Darcy a little homesick. She loved her New York life with Mark, except the job lately, but she still considered DC her home, and it pulled at her heartstrings.

Darcy and Danielle had each gotten to know Connie and Nathan Pierce in different cities but in the same year. Danielle had met them in Boston when Alex saved their son's life after a terrible traffic accident on Thanksgiving eve. Darcy had met them in DC a month later when they all attended the same Redskins football game and sat together in Mr. Snyder, the owner's, box. At the time, Darcy had been a successful and popular realtor, and Mark had become the "unofficial" voice of the team.

After meeting both identical twins and learning they hadn't spoken to each other in fifteen years, Connie tried to promote a reconciliation. She wanted them to meet and hash out their problems. However, circumstances continued to keep them apart until they finally reunited at their father's deathbed. They forgave each other for past transgressions and now were true sisters again and the best of friends.

Darcy and Danielle had regained their "twin thing," as they called the strange radar between the two. They could finish each other's sentences and were perfectly attuned to each other. That twin connection had been worrying Danielle lately. She sensed that something was bothering Darcy, and yet she couldn't get Darcy to admit anything was wrong. After tonight's celebration, she was going to sit down and have a long-overdue heart-to-heart talk.

For the past six years, the twins had lived in the same condo building in New York City. Danielle had married Dr. Alex Stone, the love of her life, and they'd had their son, Freddy, a year later. Now Danielle was pregnant again with a little girl.

Darcy and Mark, madly in love and true workaholics, continued to climb the broadcasting ladder of success together. They were inseparable and were fast becoming the most famous duo in sports broadcasting history. They were recognized and treated as celebrities everywhere and had chosen to put off having a family for now. Their Emmy-winning talk show, *Speaking of Sports with Donavan & Donavan* was their child. It consumed all their time and energy. Darcy resented that there wasn't time for anything else in her life, but Mark seemed oblivious to her worries and was blissfully happy.

After another two hours, the election results were finalized, and Senator Nathan Pierce was proclaimed the president-elect, with his inauguration set for two months away, in late January. Darcy and Danielle hugged each other and jumped up and down as tears of happiness streamed down their cheeks. Even Alex and Mark grew misty eyed when Nathan made his emotional acceptance speech from his Boston headquarters. Balloons by the dozen fell from the ceiling, and streamers flew through the air in the various election headquarters. Something wonderful was about to happen for the country with Nathan as its new leader; and although they didn't know it yet, Darcy and Danielle's lives were about to change forever.

CHAPTER 4

Danielle

Danielle arrived at Healing Words headquarters, dressed in her favorite forest green, St. John's knit business suit, and matching Louboutin spiked heels, which showed off her long, shapely legs. Her shoulder-length blonde hair was pulled back into a chic French twist. She wore gold loop earrings and a gold Cartier watch. Other than her wedding ring, they were her only accessories. She looked like a runway fashion model but with a pleasantly rounded pregnant belly.

She had the brilliant mind of a chemist. When she was at work, she was all business. Today, after running the quarterly board of directors meeting, she was prepared to tackle the ever-increasing problems of managing a rapidly expanding hospital-based self-help program.

In the beginning, when she had first conceived the idea of Healing Words, everything had been so easy. From her own financial resources, she supplied colorful spiral notebooks and pens to any patient undergoing chemo treatments at New York Hospital. Participation in her program was purely voluntary, and the patient's privacy was respected at all times.

The concept was simple. Through a wide variety of writing exercises she'd personally designed with the help of her former psychiatrist and close friend, Dr. Ray Smith, the gravely ill patients were able to express and vent their fears and frustrations on paper and then share their common problems with others in the group who were facing the same daunting circumstances. After one or two sessions, most patients found themselves bonding with each other and forming friendships that lasted long after their treatments ceased.

At first the sessions were small, seven or eight patients at a time. As the word spread about the success of the program, more and more people sought to join it. Soon satellite groups assembled in hospitals all over New York City. Danielle happily continued to supply the notebooks and lesson plans, and she personally led many of the meetings herself. She was an amazingly empathetic and a caring person because she had been through therapy herself. She understood the value of expressing one's thoughts and fears aloud and on paper while seeking solutions, even though sometimes there were no good answers.

Dr. Smith had originally acted as a consultant to Healing Words. He had helped Danielle launch the program and expand it throughout New York City and to many other hospitals nationwide. Dr. Smith was in town today to accept the position as chair of the board of directors. Danielle was thrilled that he had agreed to take the job. She trusted his judgment implicitly, and she needed someone to help her with the day-to-day problems. She couldn't handle everything by herself any longer and be a proper mother to little Freddy. Alex was always willing to be her sounding board and come to her aide; however, his days were frantically busy too. There weren't enough hours in the day. With a new baby on the way, she was overwhelmed and definitely needed help.

CHAPTER 5

Darcy

Darcy woke with a start. The alarm must have gone off, but she never heard it. She glanced anxiously around the bedroom. Mark had already gotten up and showered. She saw his wet towel hanging over the back of the bathroom door. She sprang out of bed, feeling a little groggy ... too much champagne at last night's election-night festivities.

"Mark," she called out to the empty room, "why didn't you wake me? We have to be at the airport soon." *Speaking of Sports* was broadcasting from Denver that evening for the Thursday night football game between the Broncos and the 49ers, and Darcy and Mark were scheduled to interview the opposing coaches before and after the game.

"Here, sweetheart." Mark came into the room, carrying a small tray with two cups of steaming black coffee. "I thought you might need this."

"Thanks," she said gratefully. "I guess I drank a little too much last night."

"Not so anyone would notice," he reassured her. "But when we got home, you did start babbling on and on about needing to talk to me about something important. But then you fell asleep. What is it?"

Darcy wanted to tell him about her wish to end their talk show, but this wasn't the time. They had to hurry now to get to the airport. On the plane, she'd have four uninterrupted hours to sound him out and try to convince him that it was time for them to make a career change and do something else more important with their time and money.

"Not now," she stalled. "I need to get dressed. Let's talk on the way to Denver." Before she could say anything else, the phone rang.

"I'll get it in the den," Mark offered. "You'd better shower and get ready. The town car will be here in forty minutes to pick us up."

Twenty minutes later she was standing by their duplex's front door, her overnight bag on the floor next to her. She held her purse and a briefcase stuffed full of notes about tonight's game. "Are you ready?" She looked anxiously around for her husband. "I just got a text from the driver. The car's already here."

Mark walked slowly into the foyer. His handsome face was ashen, and his eyes were open wide in disbelief. She could see his hands shaking, and his normally strong voice was unsteady. "I'm afraid we're not going anywhere."

"What do you mean? Has our flight been cancelled?" She was confused.

"Not our flight ... our show," he said in a monotone.

CHAPTER 6

Danielle

Dr. Ray Smith sat across the desk from Danielle. "I think the board meeting went very well. But there's so much to do going forward. I honestly think you'll need more help running this program than I can provide."

"Yes, I suppose so. I am not egotistical enough to think I can single-handedly manage this organization now that it's growing so quickly. I relish the idea of being able to turn some of the daily duties and responsibilities over to you."

"That's not exactly what I meant." He studied her face, trying to gauge her mood. "I know you were counting on me to be your right-hand man, but frankly, that's not logical or even possible. I promise I will certainly do everything I can to help you in my role as the chair of the board. However, I still have my practice and clinical responsibilities back in Boston. I can't devote the necessary time that running Healing Words requires. I wasn't sure how you'd feel about a suggestion I have. That's why I wanted to talk to you about it privately rather than in front of the entire board."

Danielle knew him very well. He was guarded and stalling, which was unusual. Normally he was a get-straight-to-the-point type of person. "For heaven's sake, Ray, what's this all about? You're sounding very mysterious."

"Danielle, you have done a great job in creating and expanding this wonderful program, and I don't want to hurt your feelings. I'm afraid this may be hard for you to hear, but I'm suggesting that you hire an outside executive to help you run Healing Words going forward. You are much too busy now as it is, and with the new baby coming, there's a pretty good chance that some critical details could fall between the cracks. You can't afford to take that risk with the program just as it's starting to really take off."

Danielle thought about it for a moment and reluctantly agreed. She'd been worried about how she could manage everything—the creative writing program, little Freddy, the new baby, and her marriage without short-changing something. She stressed about it constantly.

"Yes, I'm sure you're right," she said. "You of all people appreciate how many hours I've devoted to this program, but the demands are becoming more and more onerous. I used to just run into Target, buy a dozen colorful spiral notebooks, and hand them out to patients. Now I have to search the internet for the best bulk prices and fill out purchase orders. Even ordering pens and T-shirts with our logo has become an issue because we need to be completely transparent and vigilant to maintain our nonprofit tax status. I have to show how every penny is spent and justify all our expenses. The math and accounting involved are way over my pay grade. I know I need help, at least with those issues."

Dr. Smith wanted to reassure her. "I've sensed that lately you seem a bit overwhelmed. That's why I contacted a national search firm on your behalf and have already put out feelers, seeking the right candidate. Once I narrow the applicants down, I'll have them interview directly with you. Whomever you pick, be it a man or a woman, you'll have to work very closely with that person, so I want you to be completely comfortable and to have the final say. The board will support whomever you choose. All of us have such admiration for your efforts."

"That's very considerate." Danielle sighed. While she was happy to be relieved from some of the tedious day-to-day work at Healing Words, she was a little afraid of being rendered unimportant or replaced altogether. It dawned on her that she would no longer be the sole boss. Giving up some of her power would be difficult and take some getting used to. She needed to talk the matter over with Alex and let the notion settle for a few days. She hadn't fully grasped that having another child might cost her the control of her beloved program. She needed time to adjust to this new circumstance.

"Don't worry. Like in the past, I'll help you through any problems. You can always count on me," Dr. Smith said earnestly. She felt like he'd been reading her mind. He knew her so well.

She spoke tentatively. "This is going to take some getting used to. I hope I can adapt."

CHAPTER 7

Darcy

Darcy stared at Mark in disbelief. "What do you mean, our show is canceled?"

"Because …" He couldn't finish the sentence. He fell dejectedly into the hall chair and buried his face in his hands.

"Mark, my goodness! What's happened? You're scaring me." Darcy dropped her purse and briefcase, and ran to her husband's side. "You look like someone's died."

"Yes, someone did die," he answered morosely. "And that someone is me … or rather it's us, our show, *Speaking of Sports*."

"What do you mean?" She was flabbergasted. "How is that possible? What are you talking about? You're not making any sense."

Mark stood up stiffly and pulled Darcy toward the den. "We need to talk," he said. "This is catastrophic. Our careers are over."

She had never seen her husband so upset. He was shaking and suddenly seemed to have aged ten years.

"What's this all about?" She took a seat on the sofa in their den, her favorite room in their condo; it was filled with sports paraphernalia and award plaques attesting to their broadcasting expertise and the success of *Speaking of Sports*. "I don't understand any of this, Mark. You're talking in riddles."

"Honestly, I don't understand it myself." He groaned. "But that phone call was from Brad Hudson, an executive producer at the network. I don't know him very well. I think I've only seen him a half dozen times in all these years. We always deal with our own producer, Todd Fleishman. Anyway—"

Mark took a deep breath and realized he was rambling. Darcy was having difficulty following his train of thought. "Brad told me that our show's been canceled, effective immediately. The network will make an announcement in a day or two, saying that we're leaving the show to pursue other opportunities, but that's it. No further details or explanations. We get no severance pay. No vacation time. No nothing. We're toast." He buried his head in his hands again and let out an unconscious sound like an animal wail. "My ... our ... careers are over, just like that."

Darcy grabbed Mark's shaking hand. "How can that be? I still don't get it. Why was the show canceled so abruptly? We have the network's top-rated show. What happened? Does this Brad guy have the authority to fire us?"

"Apparently he does. According to him, someone has accused me of broadcasting false headline-grabbing stories to pump up our ratings."

"That's impossible! Who would say such a thing?" Darcy began to shake. She knew the charges were false. Mark would never to do anything like that. "What stories? Don't you have a chance to defend yourself?"

"Apparently not. The powers that be are keeping my accuser's name a secret supposedly to avoid reprisals from me. There are witnesses who will substantiate the claim and are willing to testify to my wrongful reporting." He slammed his fist into the sofa angrily. "It's all made-up, fake news. Darcy, believe me. How can this happen in America today? It's so blatantly unfair. I've been railroaded and never will know who did this to me ... to us ... or why."

"I'm sorry, darling. I know the show was your dream. It's totally unfair. Are you sure someone isn't playing a joke on you?" The situation didn't make any sense. "*Speaking of Sports* is the network's biggest financial success. The network would be crazy to walk away from that revenue."

"This is no joke. Brad was very clear and unapologetic. He said that in their legal department's opinion, I have egregiously violated the morals clause in my contract and that consequently, I ... rather we ... and the show are done. We are not even allowed back in the building. They will box up our stuff and send it here. It's as if this malicious charge from out of nowhere has totally erased our entire careers, and we have absolutely no recourse. Our show is done, and so are we as sportscasters."

"I don't believe that for a minute," Darcy protested, fighting back angry tears. "We need a lawyer." She had to think for both of them. Mark was too upset. "Is Bill Robinson still practicing?"

"I don't know. I haven't seen or talked to him since he settled your father's estate five years ago. But if he's retired, I'm sure he left his practice in capable hands. There'll be someone in his office who can help us," Mark responded in a dull, defeated voice. He had been crushed by the phone call and the injustice of the false allegations against him. Had the workplace become so toxic and treacherous that a man was no longer assumed innocent until proven guilty?

Darcy tenderly looked at her husband. Her heart was breaking for him. She could see that his entire world and his sterling reputation had suddenly been destroyed. She shivered with guilt when she realized she had been about to ask him to voluntarily walk away from the show and the career he loved for her own selfish reasons. Was this horrific sudden firing and the canceling of their show some kind of strange karma? A payback for something evil she'd done earlier in her life? *Be careful what you wish for.*

No matter how much she had wanted a change, a new career path, she'd never wanted *Speaking of Sports* to end like this. She'd never wanted to see her husband's reputation maliciously destroyed.

CHAPTER 8

Danielle

Since Dr. Smith had suggested that a new executive officer take over the day-to-day operations of Healing Words, Danielle had felt conflicting emotions. On one hand, she was happy to have the pressures of running the rapidly growing program removed from her shoulders. She could then devote her time and energy to organizing more lesson plans, delivering more lectures to the patients, and opening more and more sites. On the other hand, she was apprehensive and anxious about giving up her authority and control. She definitely wanted to keep her fingers on the pulse of the organization and had no intention of becoming only a figurehead.

In her many psychiatric sessions with Dr. Smith, Danielle had learned the value of expressive writing, and she wanted to pay that lesson forward. She had sacrificed a lot and put her dermatology practice on hold to pursue this dream. Her idea to help cancer patients put their thoughts—positive or negative, frightening or hopeful—on paper and then share those thoughts with like-minded people had proved to be hugely rewarding and successful. She had the testimonies of hundreds of people, who thanked her for what the program had done for them. However, over the last week, she had spent several sleepless nights worrying that a new director might not have her same goals and aspirations. She was struggling, finding it difficult to let go.

She and Alex had talked about the situation extensively, and they both agreed that because of little Freddy and the soon-to-arrive little Caroline, Danielle couldn't spread herself too thin. Motherhood had to take priority.

She had met with two potential candidates so far and didn't have good feelings about either. One was an abrasive, middle-age woman with impeccable computer skills and lots of higher-education degrees, but she showed little patience or sympathy for cancer victims. She explained that she thought the Healing Words program in its present shape coddled them too much and that a more "tough love" approach would produce better outcomes in the long run.

Danielle had vehemently disagreed and ended the interview quickly after hearing that bias. Love and empathy were exactly what her program was all about. This candidate was clearly not the right person. Danielle knew she couldn't work with her and was disappointed that Ray and the personnel agency had even bothered to arrange for the interview. It had been a waste of time.

The second candidate had been a nice enough young man, fresh out of business school with lots of studious thoughts and esoteric theories but with no practical experience. He admitted that he had never met a patient who had undergone chemotherapy or faced a life-threatening illness. Again, Danielle had to question what the recruiting firm was thinking. Why had they sent these two—in her opinion, completely inappropriate candidates—for her to evaluate? She was disappointed in their choices and planned to call a special meeting of the board as soon as possible to discuss the issue and find a different recruiting firm. In the meantime, she was going to do her best to find her own replacement.

Danielle didn't know where to begin, so she needed to use her sister as a sounding board. Maybe through her television contacts, Darcy would know someone who might be interested in the job. Danielle had been funding the entire program's expenses and the staff salaries from her own funds, so money wasn't an issue. She'd pay whatever was necessary to hire someone with good people skills, integrity, and common sense ... someone who understood the compassion behind her concept.

Danielle picked up her kitchen phone and called Darcy. "Freddy's down for his nap, and Alex is at the hospital. I really need to talk to you about something important. Can I bribe you to come down and join me for a cup of coffee? Also, I want to invite you and Mark for Thanksgiving dinner. Alex is bound and determined to fry the turkey this year. He's driving me crazy talking about it."

Darcy was loath to leave Mark alone in the apartment. He had just learned that their ESPN show was abruptly cancelled, and they were both in shock. Mark was so rattled that he could barely speak. His professional life had virtually fallen apart in the last fifteen minutes. They needed time to be together to digest what had happened and to figure out what they should do next.

"I can't come down now," Darcy spoke in a choked voice. "Our show's been canceled, and Mark is beyond devastated. We're sitting here in total disbelief. It just happened a few minutes ago. I don't know what to do or how to help him." She began to sob. "Sorry, Danielle," she stammered, "I can't talk anymore." She hung up and crumpled to the floor in despair.

CHAPTER 9

Danielle and Darcy

Danielle pounded on Darcy's door, then used her key to let herself in. "Darcy, Mark, where are you?"

Darcy ran to hug her sister. "This is so awful. We're just sitting here in shock. How could this possibly happen?" She was still furious at herself for ever thinking she should ask Mark to leave their show, now that she saw how devasted he was. Thank goodness she hadn't said anything to him about it.

Mark sat stiffly on the sofa, staring wide eyed at his Emmy statue and the numerous framed pictures of Darcy and him posed with dozens of professional athletics, team owners, and other celebrities. Trying to make himself focus on what had happened, he inhaled sharply and turned toward Danielle. "Have you talked to Bill Robinson since your father's estate was settled and he booted Karin out of the family's Fifth Avenue house?"

"Yes," Danielle answered. "He's been very helpful in setting up the financial structure for Healing Words. I'm in pretty regular contact with him. Why?"

"Because we need a lawyer to tell us where we stand, if there's anything we can do. Should we fight this atrocity and try to get our show back? My personal feeling is that I don't want to go back, even if I clear my name. Any organization that treats its people like this is not a place where I want to work. But maybe that's my foolish pride talking," Mark said angrily.

"No, it's not. I don't want the job back either," Darcy stated righteously. "If this is the way those bastards reward our loyalty and hard work, we certainly aren't going to force our way back in, even if we legally can."

"I want nothing more to do with television. But I want to know who's behind this, who made these false allegations, and who the anonymous witness is," Mark replied emphatically.

Darcy explained to Danielle what had happened that morning, and Mark filled her in about what had been said on the phone call with the executive producer. Mark was seething with anger, but the hurt and disillusion he felt were plainly visible on his face.

"I don't understand how something like this dismissal can happen. This is America, for God's sake. What happened to innocent before proven guilty?" Danielle was outraged and full of empathy for her sister and her brother-in-law. They didn't deserve this insult. They were both such decent people. She wished there was something she could do to help.

"I think in this age of sexual harassment, teenage sex trafficking, and every other sordid thing that goes on, the networks and corporate America executives prefer to cut their problems loose, like a flailing fish on a line, and hope that fish doesn't come back to bite them," Darcy answered. "They are looking for the simplest and fastest way out of any bad situation."

"Or something like that." Mark smiled in spite of his anguish. Darcy always came up with the funniest analogies. This one wasn't great, but she was partially right, and he understood what she meant.

"Many successful careers have been ruined by false accusations," Mark said soberly. "Look at what they tried to do to Judge Kavanaugh. I'm not going to let some anonymous evil person ruin mine. I'm going to fight for my good name, but fuck the damn job."

"And I'm right beside you." Darcy went over to her husband, took hold of him, and hugged him fiercely. "As always, it's Donavan and Donavan together."

"Alex and I will be right here with you too," Danielle said earnestly. "Nobody's going to push you and my sister around. Between the four of us, and with Mr. Robinson's help, we'll get to the bottom of this issue, and believe me, someone's going to pay." She pulled out her phone and searched for the lawyer's number. "Here." She handed Mark her phone. "Call him now."

Darcy smiled gratefully at her sister. She was thankful that Danielle had barged in and forced them to do something besides sit around and wring their hands. Darcy was usually the strongest of the two twins, but today she had needed her sister to take charge, and Danielle had.

Danielle had become a really strong woman since her sessions with Dr. Smith back in Boston. She was no longer a pushover and had definite, well-thought-out opinions and beliefs of her own. She no longer lived in Darcy's shadow and nowadays was a person in her own right. It was wonderful to see, and Darcy needed her support now more than ever.

The baby monitor Danielle had clipped to her skirt beeped, and she could hear and see Freddy stirring in his crib. "Sorry, I've got to go," she apologized. "My little man is waking up and will want his snack." She hugged Mark and Darcy, and left promptly to tend to her son.

When she was back in her own apartment and Freddy was happily enjoying milk and cookies, she remembered that she'd wanted to speak to Darcy about her fears for the future of Healing Words and the search for an executive assistant. *Oh well, one problem at a time*, she thought. Hers could wait until Darcy and Mark had gotten some answers about their own dilemma.

Maybe there was something she could do. She realized she had left her cell phone upstairs with Mark and Darcy, so she grabbed the landline in the kitchen instead and began dialing.

CHAPTER 10

Darcy

Darcy and Mark arrived the next day at Mr. Robinson's law offices on the sixty-fifth floor of a downtown Manhattan building. They remembered that the previous time they'd been there, shortly after Darcy's father's death, had been for the reading of his will. It had been a remarkable day when the girls' haughty stepmother, Karin, had finally been put in her place and Mr. Robinson had informed her that she was now penniless and would have to leave the family home before she was evicted. Danielle and Darcy, not normally vindictive, had been thrilled that Karin was finally made to suffer after all the pain she had caused them and their father. Neither of the twins had given her another thought. She was dead to them.

Looking around the familiar room, Mark and Darcy immediately felt at home in the tastefully decorated reception area with its dark-wood floors, emerald-green oriental rug, rich chocolate leather sofas, and portraits of the law firm's partners hanging on the walls. The room reeked of old money and tradition. A pleasant receptionist came over to them to offer coffee or water, which they politely refused. Mr. Robinson didn't keep them waiting long.

"How nice to see you both again." He greeted them warmly and led them down a long corridor to his corner office. "I do get to see Danielle from time to time. And you, girls—excuse me, you two beautiful young *women*—get lovelier with every passing year."

"Thank you." Darcy blushed. She liked her father's lawyer and felt comfortable with him. "It's nice to see you again too. Unfortunately, this is not a social call. I'm afraid we badly need your legal advice."

"I suspected as much." He had seen the newspapers and was curious about their sudden departure from their hit television show, *Speaking of Sports with Donavan & Donavan*. The articles were complimentary and thanked the couple for their excellent work and for changing the way sports news was delivered. The network said they would be missed and wished them well with their new endeavors. But too much had been left unsaid. What new endeavors? Over the years, he had read about or seen other well-publicized but distinctly hasty departures from high-powered jobs. Usually that signaled a more complicated, intriguing underlying story.

"I'm all ears," he said and pulled out his iPad to make notes. "Tell me what this is all about."

CHAPTER 11

Danielle

Danielle was stirring the sauce for the lasagna. She couldn't get Darcy's problem out of her mind but had been so busy getting ready for tonight's visiting-professor dinner that she hadn't told Alex about Darcy and Mark's canceled show and the unfounded allegations against Mark.

She and Alex were expecting fifteen medical residents for tonight's regular Wednesday dinner at their home. The evenings had become a tradition for the medical students, residents, and the fellows Alex taught during their surgical rotations at the hospital. The students eagerly anticipated the informal gatherings, and it was a learning and social occasion for all of them. Danielle and Alex had been hosting these weekly nights for the last five years and looked forward to the dialogue and comradery they fostered.

Danielle felt a little queasy as she added the sausage and ground beef to the sauce but chewed on a saltine and kept preparing the meal. The table was set, and Freddy was running around with his little white chef's hat sitting atop his curly hair. He loved these evenings because his parents let him stay up long enough to welcome the guests. It was his assignment to stand next to the statue of Hippocrates at the front door and hold the evening's menu, which he proudly handed out. The guests loved to see him and giggled at how seriously Freddy took his job.

The guests filed into the apartment, one after another, and the conversation quickly became lively and informative. Every week these special dinners consisted of the medical students, residents and fellows. There was always a special guest of honor, a distinguished medical faculty member or a renowned physician or scientist, who would lecture the next day at the hospital for "Grand Rounds." The students loved the opportunity to meet with these famous people and have one-on-one interactions.

Alex had dreamed up the idea for these dinners when he first came to New York. He believed they helped the students feel comfortable with him as a teacher, and he was always looking for different ways to share his vast medical knowledge and expertise with them. He enjoyed mentoring, and lately he was spending more and more time with them. He missed the old days of trauma surgery and the thrill of saving lives, but he had accepted what life dealt him and made the best of it. He loved teaching and being around the students. He said it made him feel young again and useful.

Danielle loved the evenings too. She didn't mind the extra work involved or the cooking. They were her way of helping Alex, and he loved her all the more for them. She never complained, even now when she wasn't feeling great and was carrying the equivalent of a basketball around on her stomach. Danielle learned a lot from the students and carefully listened to them express their anxieties about finishing their rotations or passing exams and finding good jobs after they graduated. She often incorporated their reflections into her materials at Healing Words. Coping with worry and uncertainty was the same, whether it was produced from a life-threatening disease or general fears about the future.

As she was serving the coffee and Alex was dishing out the apple pie, the phone rang. Normally Danielle wouldn't answer it when she had company, but she recognized the number on her caller ID. "Excuse me," she said to Alex and her guests. "I have to take this." She stepped into the hallway.

"Hi," Ray Smith greeted her warmly. "I hope I'm not disturbing you, but I think I've found exactly the right person to be your executive director, and I'd like to bring him to meet you as soon as possible."

"Who?" Danielle was curious. She still wasn't completely comfortable with turning her program over to someone else to run, and she hadn't cared for the other two candidates.

"His name is Don March. He's forty-five, a former colleague of mine from Duke University Medical School, and he's looking for something different to do with his life. He's been practicing psychotherapy in Durham, North Carolina. Sadly, his wife died two years ago, and now he feels it's time to make a change. I think his skills and compassion make him the perfect person. I told him all about you and Healing Words. He's very interested, wants to meet you, and has a lot of questions. Can you see us this week?"

"Absolutely. If you really think this is the right guy."

He could hear the tension in her voice. "Yes, I'm one hundred percent certain. Take a deep breath and relax." He knew her and her insecurities so well. "Trust me, Danielle. This man is going to change your life."

CHAPTER 12

Darcy

Darcy and Mark walked back to their apartment after meeting with Mr. Robinson. They were both exhausted because they had hardly slept in days, constantly tossing and turning in bed, wondering who would think up and carry out such a hateful act. Mentally they had gone through the name of every person who worked at the studio, the staff in the front office and even the sponsors. They could think of no one who was that evil or vindictive. What was the motive for someone to ruin Mark's life? Not knowing their accuser was the worst part. It weighed heavily on them. Mr. Robinson had promised to help find the perpetrator but warned them that the process would be costly and time consuming.

"That was quite a lot to digest," Mark said wearily. "I'm no clearer now on what we should do than I was before the meeting. I can't decide if it's worth the time and money to fine the culprit. Maybe we should simply cut our losses and try to move on. Otherwise this might end up eating us alive."

"Let's have lunch and talk about it some more later. I'm a bit confused. There are pros and cons, no matter what we decide to do."

"I'd like to talk to Alex when he gets home today. He's got a level head, and I think he can help us make an unemotional decision. Danielle too, if she's got time."

"I know she'll make time for us," Darcy said, "but she mentioned earlier today that she had an important interview with some doctor from

Duke. She expected to be at her office with him all afternoon. Actually, she was a little mysterious about the whole thing. I have no idea what it's all about."

Mark went into the kitchen and began rummaging through the refrigerator and pantry for some salad ingredients. "What kind of dressing?" he called out to her.

"Surprise me," she answered and picked up the house phone, which had started to ring.

"Hi, Nathan. It's so nice to hear from you. Yes, he's right here." She handed the phone to Mark. "It's Nathan." The two couples hadn't spoken since election night. Darcy had missed her daily chats with Connie, but she had been too upset to talk to her friend about the show's cancellation.

"Hi there, Mr. President-Elect. How's it going for you and Connie in DC?" Mark began to whisk together a lemon vinaigrette dressing. Whenever he was stressed, cooking was the best medicine and always calmed him down.

"Can you put me on speaker please so Darcy can hear this conversation too?" Nathan asked. "What I have to say involves you both."

Mark pressed the button. "We're both on the line now. What's up?"

"Well, as you know, Connie and I are supposed to be putting together our White House staffs and selecting names that I'd like to propose for my cabinet. It's serious business and a bit intimidating. I need to be careful about my selections and be as sure as possible that my nominations will be approved when the time comes. I don't want to endure endless confirmation proceedings and wrangling with the press about their qualifications or teenage drinking habits."

"Sure, of course not." Mark answered, not sure why Nathan was telling him all this. But he was always happy to talk to his friend. "Is there anything I can do to help?"

"Yes, that's why I'm calling. I need someone I really trust to be my voice here at the White House, to be my face to the media. I can't think of a better communicator than you, Mark. You handle the mic better than anyone I've ever seen, and people like and trust you.

"I know this is coming completely out of the blue," he continued, "but I read that the two of you left your network show rather abruptly.

That's terrific news for me, because I want very much to offer you the job as my press secretary. It would mean you'd have to move back to DC right away, but as I recall, you kept your Massachusetts Avenue condo here when you and Darcy moved to New York City."

Darcy and Mark couldn't believe what they were hearing. They looked at each other in utter astonishment. Was Nathan being serious? Mark working in the White House?

"I—I don't know what to say," Mark stammered. "I have never pictured myself in politics. I am speechless."

"Well, that's a terrible quality for a press secretary." Nathan chuckled. "You have to be able to think on your feet at all times if you're going to be my spokesperson. I warn you, it's a tough and often thankless job, and it doesn't pay so well either. That being said, I know you can handle the job, and I'd really like to have you in my corner."

Mark looked at Darcy, stunned and yet intrigued by Nathan's surprise offer.

"I think you'll be the perfect person for the job." Darcy smiled at her husband without hesitation. "This job at this time is an absolute gift from God."

"Can we have a little time to think this over?" Mark asked, still in shock over the offer. "It'll be quite an upheaval, and I want to be sure Darcy is really on board, because as you know, first and foremost we're a team."

"Yes. Of course. You can have the whole rest of the day to decide." He laughed. "But seriously, the reason I wanted Darcy on the line is because Connie's tied up at some congressional woman's function and asked me to speak on her behalf. If you agree, Darcy, she'll talk to you more specifically when she gets home later this evening."

"Agree to do what?" Darcy had no idea what he was talking about.

"Connie would like to offer Darcy the job as her personal private assistant. Basically, Darcy, you would work with Connie's chief of staff... also yet to be named. You would help make all Connie's appointments, approve and arrange her social calendar, spearhead her pet projects, and coordinate her travel plans. You would also work very closely with my own chief of staff, who's yet to be determined ... and with my sister, the indomitable Ginger Gardner." Nathan chuckled. "I know you love her and she you. My bossy sister wants to run the social end of things here at the White House. Connie's so busy that she's okay with that for now if Darcy's here to bring some common sense to the table. It will be a huge relief for my wife not to have to deal with my opinionated sister all the time and to leave social affairs to you two capable women."

Darcy clapped her hands together in excitement and started jumping up and down. Working in the White House would be a dream come true, and she had wanted to spend more time with Ginger anyway. This would be the perfect opportunity, and they'd be going home to Washington.

"Connie and I believe you and Darcy can handle these two difficult jobs, and it would be so reassuring to have Donavan and Donavan working side by side on the Pierce administration team. What do you say?"

For a few seconds there wasn't a sound in the room. Then Darcy let out a shriek of glee. "Yes, yes. Tell Connie I'm all in but only if Mark agrees." She looked at her husband and saw the gleam had returned to his eyes. He was suddenly standing straighter and looked more like his old self. With this new opportunity and a move back to Washington, they could put the nightmare at the network behind them and move forward with a whole new, exciting life … and in the city they both adored and had fallen in love with.

"Well?" Darcy looked pleadingly at her husband, holding her breath and crossing her fingers. "What's your decision? The president-elect and First Lady are waiting for your answer."

CHAPTER 13

Danielle

Danielle impatiently looked at her watch. She was anxious to meet Don March and secretly hoped she wouldn't like him. She was still struggling with turning Healing Words over to someone else to run. If she kept finding fault with all the potential candidates, she could delay the transition. On the other hand, she was realistic enough to know it would be better for the program to have the new person in place before she went on maternity leave.

A knock on her office door signaled Dr. Smith's arrival. "Danielle, I want you to meet my good friend, Dr. Don March."

Don stepped out from behind Dr. Smith. He arched his eyebrows and appeared to be scrutinizing Danielle. He hadn't expected her to be so young or quite so attractive, even though she was clearly very pregnant. "Thanks for taking this meeting," he said. "I've been looking forward to this little chat."

Little chat? Danielle looked aghast and took a step backward behind the security of her desk. Turning her program over to a complete stranger wasn't happening after "a little chat," she thought angrily. *Who does this pompous jerk think he is?* Don March was making it easy for her to dislike him. She wasn't turning Healing Words over to someone like him. Danielle took a deep breath, inhaled deeply, and tried to compose herself.

"Dr. March." She frowned her disapproval. "I believe Dr. Smith has explained our program to you in depth and our current need for some more help. He said you expressed interest in our position as executive director. I was under the impression that you had some questions for me."

She noticed that his eyes were darting all around the room, taking in every detail, but he was avoiding looking directly at her. That fact made Danielle uncomfortable. She liked a man who looked her in the eyes when he spoke. Don March wasn't particularly handsome. His face had sharp, well-defined features; his hair was a bit unruly, and his smile was a little crooked. He hadn't taken the time to shave. He had a four o'clock shadow, and it was barely 11:00 a.m. Did his manner show arrogance or disrespect? Dr. March was taller than Danielle in her high heels but not by much. His physical appearance didn't appeal to her, and neither did his personality. He made her uncomfortable.

"Please take a seat." Danielle signaled to the two men. "Let's talk."

"I think I'll leave the talking to the two of you," Dr. Smith said succinctly. "I have other board business to tend to this morning. I'll check back in with you two later." He winked at Danielle and silently mouthed the words "Be nice" before leaving the office. He could see Don had ruffled her delicate feathers, but he would leave it to the two of them to resolve their differences.

Dan took a chair opposite Danielle and made himself comfortable. He sat back casually, crossed one knee over the other and acted as if he was in charge in his own office and she was the visitor. Something about his mannerisms made her anxious. He was too cocky. He didn't seem to realize *she* was the one conducting the interview. He appeared to believe he already had the job. She had been around other self-assured, cocky physicians, and rather than impress her, their boorish behavior turned her off.

"My first question," he blurted out with no preamble, "is, who will have the final say if we should find ourselves at odds about something?" Don March wasn't a man of diplomacy.

"I haven't really thought that through," she stated, embarrassed that she had no good answer for him. She felt her face heat up and her cheeks turn red. "I guess I assumed that whoever took the job would work with me as my equal partner—you know, be on the same page about major issues. I wasn't anticipating problems or power struggles."

The more she talked, the more imbecilic she sounded to herself. He had put her on the defensive. She grimaced when she realized how juvenile she sounded and was mortified that she'd given him the upper hand. She obviously hadn't thought this new relationship through carefully enough. To be fair, it wasn't his fault she was so unprepared.

"That's a little naive, don't you think?" he said. "How can you expect any sane person to take a job where there's no clear lines of authority ... no chain of command? It's ludicrous." He looked her squarely in the eye this time. "If I were to accept this job, I would need full autonomy."

You arrogant SOB, Danielle thought. She was astounded by his brassy words. The job hadn't been offered to him, nor would it be, if she had her way. The silence in the room was deafening. She couldn't possibly work with this arrogant, self-centered man with his super-inflated ego. *What is Ray Smith thinking?*

"I think I've heard enough," Danielle said dismissively, standing up. "Thank you for coming, but I don't think this is going to work for me. Good day, Dr. March."

CHAPTER 14

Darcy

Darcy twirled around in their den in utter ecstasy. "I can't believe we're going back to Washington. Just when things looked so bleak here, out of the blue Nathan called and offered us the jobs of a lifetime. Now we'll be working together in the White House … and with the 'Gin Bottle] too (her affectionate nickname for Ginger Gardner). It's almost as if our guardian angel whispered in Nathan's ears about us."

"It's hard to fathom," Mark readily agreed. "It's so totally unexpected but fabulous."

"You're happy? Right?" she asked. "You really want to go back to Washington?"

She held her breath, waiting for his answer. Mark had been devastated by what had happened at the network, and Darcy hoped he wasn't grasping at straws by accepting this new position so quickly. Neither of them had enough time to digest and cope with what had happened. She knew they should spend more time processing it all and trying to figure out who had accused Mark. But now that wasn't going to be an option. Nathan and Connie needed them in Washington right away.

Although she knew Mark would be perfect for the job, Darcy didn't want him to regret the move later on. Broadcasting had always been his life. Instead of talking for himself and bantering with her, he would now be on the opposite side of the microphone, speaking for someone else. Would he be happy doing that?

"I'm overwhelmed," Mark answered soberly. "My mind's spinning with all the arrangements we'll have to make in such a short time. I guess I can leave those details to you."

Then he had an "aha moment." "How do you think Danielle will take this news? And right before her baby is due. She was depending on you to be here to help out. This move of ours will be very hard on her."

"Oh My God. I hadn't thought about that. She'll miss us terribly, and I know she'll be very upset that we're leaving New York, but after what happened at work here, I know she'll support our decision. Alex will be happy for us too. They have enough money that they can afford to hire a full-time nanny … two if need be. This move of ours will give them a good excuse to come to DC to visit us and to see Connie and Nathan more often too. I think everything will work out in the long run."

Darcy paused for a moment and reflected more soberly on Danielle. She and her identical twin sister were so close. They looked and spoke exactly alike and were together constantly. They had always been able to read each other's mind and finish the other's sentence. It was one of the magnificent benefits of the "twin connection." Since reconciling at their father's deathbed after a torturous fifteen-year estrangement, they had become closer now than ever. Deliberately putting so many miles between them would be a hardship on both girls but particularly on Danielle in the last months of her difficult pregnancy. Darcy took a deep breath and silently prayed, *Let Danielle be okay about this move, dear God.*

Mark interrupted her thoughts. "Well then, since we've agreed to do this, we'd better start making arrangements. What do you want to do with this condo? Should we sell it?"

"No, please," Darcy begged. "I love our home here. We can afford to keep it, and I know it will make Danielle feel better, knowing we still own in the building. It'll be nice to have our home to stay in, instead of a hotel, when we come back for holidays or weekends."

"That's pretty optimistic," Mark answered. "I think the White House is going to keep us both pretty damn busy. I doubt we'll be able to get back here very often, at least not in the beginning. But I agree. Let's keep it. Our condo in DC is fully furnished. All we really have to do is pack some clothes and a few odds and ends. Mr. Robertson can handle the network mess for us, and Alex can check in on this apartment from time to time. Actually, this move will be quite easy."

"I'd better call the management company in DC and let them know we're coming back next week. I'll arrange for them to hire a cleaning crew to come in, and I'll order some groceries online and have them delivered. By this time next week, you'll feel like we never left." Darcy had a sudden thought and smiled mischievously. "Do you think with Nathan's connections we can get our hands on some Redskin tickets?"

"I'll see what I can do. And remember, I have loads of connections myself. The bastard who had us fired may have stolen our jobs, but he can't take away our friends and family." He took her in his arms and squeezed her tightly. "Honey, thank you for going along with all these changes. I know its sudden, and I realize how much you'll miss your sister and little Freddy. But you know, we really do make a great team. We hadn't planned on this unexpected turn of events, but it seems that Donavan and Donavan are about to hit the road again. This time it's down I-95 to Washington, DC … 1600 Pennsylvania Avenue."

CHAPTER 15

Darcy and Danielle

Danielle pounded loudly on Darcy's door. She held Freddy in one arm and a glass of flavored water in her other hand. "Sorry to intrude, but I am so damn angry. Am I interrupting anything? I am so mad that I have to vent, and Alex won't be home for a while."

Darcy studied her sister. Danielle was normally very calm and composed, but something was clearly bothering her. Her face was flushed and not from carrying Freddy.

"Put Freddy down, and I'll get him something to play with. This is great timing. Mark and I have some important news to share with you too."

Once Freddy was happily engaged with a large wooden puzzle and Mark and Darcy had their wine, Danielle began. "I told you that Ray Smith suggested that I find an executive director for Healing Words to take the pressure off me and allow me more family time."

Darcy nodded. "Yes, you mentioned that. I think that's a reasonable suggestion, but we never got a chance to talk about what that would truly mean for you going forward."

"I know," Danielle apologized. "I've been very distracted since Ray mentioned it. At first, I felt that getting some administrative help for me was a great idea, but the more I thought about it, the more reluctant I became to turn everything I'd worked so hard to accomplish over to a stranger. It means stepping away from my dream, and that scares me."

"But surely you would stay involved in some significant way," Mark said. "Danielle, it doesn't have to be all or nothing."

"That's what I was hoping also, but when Ray brought his top candidate, his friend, Dr. Don March, to meet me this afternoon, I got the distinct impression that the guy wants total control, and I'm just supposed to be a figurehead. I found him rude and arrogant. He referred to today's very important meeting, discussing the future of my program, as 'a little chat.' I was furious. He was obnoxious and treated me like a child, not as an equal. I'm a doctor too, and a damn good one, but I don't think he even acknowledged that fact. He was insufferable."

"And how do you really feel about him?" Darcy tried to lighten the moment and make a joke, but she could see her sister was getting more upset as she relayed the details of the meeting.

"He has all the necessary qualifications on paper; as a matter of fact, his credentials are quite impressive. And unfortunately, Ray Smith is solidly in his corner. However, something about the man rubs me the wrong way. He has an ego a mile long. I don't think I would ever be comfortable being in the same room, much less working with him."

"Wow, that's quite a statement." Darcy looked at her twin incredulously. "You don't usually have such negative reactions about people. I suppose you'll have to trust your instincts on this one. You didn't hire him, I presume?"

"Most certainly not." Danielle took a long gulp of her water. "I ended the interview abruptly and told him it wasn't going to work out."

"What did he say?" Mark was curious. He rarely saw Danielle so worked up.

"I don't know. I didn't hang around long enough to find out. I left the office in a huff and came right here to talk to you guys. And I'm so glad I did. I feel much better getting it off my chest. I don't know what I'd do without you both." She watched Freddy slip a puzzle piece into its correct place and remembered what Darcy had said. "Sorry to have rambled on and on like a maniac. What's your important news?"

"Well." Darcy stood up, prepared to break the news. "We got a phone call from Nathan Pierce earlier today, and—" Before she could finish her sentence, Danielle's cell phone rang.

"Sorry," Danielle mouthed to Darcy and answered the call. "Hi, sweetheart, what's up?" She spoke softly to Alex and had already put the upsetting meeting with Don March out of her mind. Just hearing her husband's voice calmed her. She adored him; he was her rock.

"Can your news wait?" she asked Darcy anxiously. "Alex ran into an old colleague a little while ago and wants to bring him home for dinner tonight. I have to run downstairs and concoct something quickly. I've become quite the short-order cook since moving to New York."

"Sure. Our news can wait a few hours," Darcy replied with relief. She was happy she could take a little more time before she had to tell her sister they were moving. As upset as Danielle was about her meeting with Dr. Don March, she didn't need any more bad news tonight. Tomorrow over coffee would be soon enough.

"Let Freddy stay with us for a while so you can set the table and prepare dinner. We'll bring him down in an hour or two," Darcy suggested. She wanted to spend time with her adorable nephew while she still could.

"Okay, thanks." Danielle kissed Freddy and hurried downstairs to prepare for their dinner guest.

CHAPTER 16

Danielle

Danielle gave Freddy his dinner and got him dressed in his Superman pajamas. She had already set the dining room table for three, draped one of Alex's Massachusetts General Hospital ties around Hippocrates's neck, and busied herself in the kitchen preparing dinner. She was so used to having company, from the years of preparing the Wednesday-night dinners for the medical students, that her freezer was fully stocked with a variety of delicious casseroles she had made in advance. She pulled out a chicken stroganoff and set it in the microwave to defrost. Then she prepared green beans with almonds and put together a salad.

She changed from her business suit into a comfortable pair of tweed slacks and a silk blouse. She was reading a bedtime story to Freddy when Alex walked in.

"Hi, honey," he greeted her warmly and high fived Hippocrates. "Nice tie," he joked to the statue and went over to hug his son. "Thanks for doing this on such short notice."

"No problem." She was always happy to support Alex. He was a wonderful husband, and she loved him unconditionally. He had literally saved her life a few years earlier when she had been severely depressed and accidentally overdosed on sleeping pills. Dr. Ray Smith had been her psychiatrist at the time. He and Alex had brought her back from that darkness, and she had been fully recovered and grateful to them both ever since.

"I was leaving the hospital when I ran into an old medical school chum. As interns, we spent a lot of time together, but then we lost touch. I believe he went somewhere in the south to do his residency, and I, of course, stayed up north at Harvard with you. He was a terrific guy back then, and I know you'll like him. We didn't have any time to talk, so we'll get caught up over dinner. Come to think of it, I don't even know why he was at the hospital."

"Any friend of yours is a friend of mine." She laughed. This wasn't the first time Alex had brought unexpected company home. Alex was a people collector. It didn't matter what a person's social status was; if you were a nice person, Alex would befriend you.

"How about I put our little man to bed, and you make us both a drink?" he offered.

"That's a deal." She headed toward the wine refrigerator and brought out a bottle of Malbec and some sparkling water for herself. She didn't know what their guest would want to drink, but they had all kinds of wine and a fully stocked bar. She placed a cheese platter and some cocktail peanuts on the coffee table and waited for Alex to return.

"Freddy's out like a light." Alex smiled. He picked up his wine glass and munched on a cracker smothered with Brie cheese. "And how was your day, sweetheart? You were interviewing a candidate for Healing Words, weren't you?"

"Yes," she replied without enthusiasm, "and he was a disaster. Not at all the kind of man I want to work with. He was condescending and pretentious. I can't believe he and Ray are friends. They are so different. After that atrocious meeting, I think I need to completely rethink this whole executive director thing. Maybe I should simply hire someone in the interim just to cover me when I'm on my maternity leave but not make it a permanent position. I don't mean to brag, but I honestly don't believe I will ever find anyone who will share my passion for Healing Words or nurture the program the way I have."

"You may be right but please be patient and keep looking. But as to this friend of Ray's, if you can't get along with him, it's his loss. He must be a real asshole."

Alex totally supported Danielle. His wife was the nicest and most compassionate person he knew. "Do what you think is best," he encouraged her. "Healing Words is your baby, and I don't want to see anyone ruin it for you."

Before he could say anything more, the doorbell rang. "I'll get it." He jumped up to welcome their dinner guest. After a warm greeting and a bear hug between the two men, Alex moved aside so he could introduce his friend to his wife.

"Danielle, this is my old friend, Don March. Don, meet the love of my life, my gorgeous wife, Danielle."

CHAPTER 17

The Dinner

Danielle froze in place. Dr. Don March, the pretentious oaf, was standing right there in her foyer. How could Alex have ever thought this jerk was such a great guy? Leopards don't change their spots. She was mortified and didn't want to have anything to do with the man. Although it was no comfort to Danielle, she could see Dr. March looked as equally rattled as she was at the strange coincidence and that he was distinctly ill at ease.

Alex, oblivious to the undercurrents of tension in the room, jovially welcome Don to their home and offered to fix him a drink. "Take a seat, Don," he said warmly. "Get to know my wonderful Danielle, and I'll be right back with your martini." He indicated Don should sit on the sofa next to the place where Danielle stood stiff and erect as an upright corpse.

"Well, this is certainly an interesting development." Don spoke to Danielle in a whisper and glanced around to be sure Alex was out of earshot.

"*Interesting* is one word for it," she muttered angrily and sat down quickly so as not to look like a stupid statue standing there. She grabbed her sparkling water from the coffee table and gulped down a healthy swig of it. "How do you propose we handle this awkward situation?"

"I don't know. I'm at a loss for words, but I don't think we have to make a big deal about it. We got off to a bad start this afternoon. That's all." He shifted nervously on the sofa and waited for her response.

A "bad start" is a gross understatement. The whole interview experience had been horrible. "I think maybe you should make up an excuse and leave. Maybe feign a headache or pretend to become suddenly ill."

"That's a bit of an overreaction, don't you think?" He seemed amused by her discomfort.

There he goes again, putting me down. This man is insufferable. How had he come to be sitting in her living room?

"Frankly," he said, ignoring her suggestion to leave, "from the way Ray Smith described your accomplishments with Healing Hands, I was expecting to meet a much older workaholic type, with black-laced, school-principal shoes, and a pencil up her ass ... not a runway model with the most amazing green eyes I've ever seen." He winked at her shocked face.

Danielle choked on her water. This man had absolutely no filter. She wondered what he'd say if she had given him the job, how he'd ever be able to handle the thorny interactions with sick cancer patients. He was a psychiatrist after all. Didn't he understand how his words affected people and that words had consequences? He couldn't always blurt out the first thought that came into his mind. Life wasn't a Rorschach test.

Danielle began practiced her yoga breathing technique to calm down. She breathed in and out slowly as she'd been taught. This man really pushed her buttons. "I was taken aback by you," she finally admitted. "I thought you were rude and were putting me down with those nasty cracks about having a 'little chat' and the 'chain of command.' I'm very proud of my expressive writing program and wasn't prepared to defend it or myself to you. I was supposed to be the one conducting the interview ... and I emphasize the word *interview*, not chat."

"I guess I did come across as rude. I apologize." This time he looked her squarely in the eye and appeared sincere. "I was nervous and trying too hard to make a good impression. I wanted to show you I'm a take-charge kind of person. I suppose I went overboard. I know it's a lot to ask, but could we pretend today never happened? I'm willing to come back to your office tomorrow morning, and we can start the interview process all over again. I'd really like the chance to show you I'm the right person for the job." He hadn't realized until now how much he wanted—no, needed—the job and how very much he'd like to work closely with her ... the chain of command be damned.

"Here's your martini." Alex came back into the room, unaware of the drama unfolding, and handed the glass to Don. "Did you two have a chance to get acquainted?"

"Yes, we're getting along just fine." Don smiled hesitantly and raised his glass to Danielle in a toast. "It's a pleasure to meet you, Danielle. My friend, Alex, is a lucky man."

"I'm so happy. I knew you'd like my wife," Alex stated proudly. "Everyone does."

Danielle, wrestling with a mix of conflicted emotions and unable to think of how to answer Don, stood up abruptly, declaring, "Dinner is served."

CHAPTER 18

Darcy

Darcy arrived at Danielle's early the next morning. "I need to talk to you. Are you free?"

"Sure. I don't have to leave for work for another hour." *Work*, she thought skeptically. That meant another interview with Don March, and she was still conflicted about him. After the initial glitch, the dinner the previous evening had gone surprising well. Alex and Don had reminisced about their medical training, shared stories, and bantered back and forth. It actually had turned into a fun night. Danielle had relaxed and allowed herself to enjoy the evening.

Don told them about his professional and personal life in Durham and about the heart-wrenching death of his wife and newborn daughter following complications from childbirth. Both his wife and their baby daughter had died within hours of each other a little over two years ago. His eyes misted as he spoke her name, Rachelle, and of the baby they'd planned to call Carly. Both Danielle and Alex had been moved by the story and could see Don was still grieving and in pain.

It was because of Don's personal, unfathomable loss that when Dr. Smith mentioned the possible position in New York, Don had jumped at the chance to interview for the job. He was intrigued with Danielle's expressive writing program because he had begun a diary of his own shortly after burying his family. Writing in it had helped him, and he saw the potential for Danielle's program to reach a much larger audience than just cancer victims. The whole world needed better coping mechanisms. The possibilities were endless.

After that sober conversation, Don switched gears, and the two men talked about a lot of different subjects. Alex and Don, who both enjoyed telling stories, exchanged hilarious jokes, and the evening that had started out with such strain and tension ended with laughter and comradery.

Danielle saw a different side of Don March. She sat back for most of the dinner, listening intently to this enigma of a man. By the end of the evening, she found herself liking him immensely and thought perhaps she had overreacted. She decided she was willing to give him a second chance. As if this morning's fiasco "chat" had never happened, she briefly explained her expressive writing program to him over dessert and inquired whether he'd be interested in interviewing for the executive director's job at Healing Words. He had appeared surprised by her overture but readily agreed. Alex applauded Danielle's suggestion and thought bringing Dan on board was a terrific idea. Danielle wasn't sure why she had kept the earlier disastrous interview a secret from her husband, but she didn't mention it then or ever.

Darcy waltzed into Danielle's kitchen and immediately picked up little Freddy. "How's my favorite nephew? I'm going to miss you, little tyke."

"Good," Freddy crooned to his aunt. "Freddy good."

"Freddy is good," Danielle lovingly corrected her son. "What's this about missing him? Are you and Mark planning a trip?"

"No, more like a four- to eight-year move to DC to work in the White House."

"What?" Danielle was flabbergasted. "You're kidding, right?"

"No, I'm not." Darcy couldn't hide her enthusiasm. "Out of nowhere, Nathan called and offered Mark the position of White House press secretary, and Connie wants me to be her personal assistant. Can you believe it? We accepted on the spot." She looked at her sister with concern. "I understand this move of ours will be hard on you, and it's going to be difficult for me too. I'll miss all our wonderful times together and of course this little munchkin." She patted Freddy's head affectionately.

"But it's such an honor and opportunity that we felt we couldn't say no. It is the White House, after all!"

"Oh, my God." Danielle sat down on the kitchen stool with a thud. The realization of what she'd initiated with one impulsive phone call to Connie smacked her in the face. "I understand it's a chance of a lifetime, but I'm selfish enough to want you guys to stay here. How am I going to manage without you? And what about the baby? You won't get to know Caroline or watch her growing up every day."

She patted her bloated stomach and choked back a sob. "This is so weird. I should be so happy for you guys, and yet I'm so sad for me at the same time."

Danielle had never expected this outcome when in confidence she had called Connie and told her what had happened at the network. She'd asked her whether she knew anyone at Fox Sports or CBS who might be willing to hire Mark and Darcy. She'd never dreamed the president and his wife would offer them jobs in their administration, which would entail a move to Washington.

The twins stood up and hugged each other tightly, laughing and crying and making plans to visit back and forth. There were so many decisions to be made and not much time. It was getting late, and Danielle realized she was going to be late for work and her appointment with Don March.

"I have to go," Danielle said reluctantly. "I have an important business matter to handle this morning, or I'd stay home with you. I had wanted to talk to you about a situation at work, but I think I resolved it last night … and certainly your news trumps mine. When will you be leaving?" she asked. "Surely not before Caroline is born in February."

"In three days, I'm afraid," Darcy said guiltily. "I know it's sudden, but we have to report for duty this Monday. We'll pack up a few things and drive to DC on Saturday. Time is of the essence, according to Nathan. He wants us to be in town to work as part of his transition team."

"So soon?" Danielle was shocked. "What about Thanksgiving and Alex's fried turkey? And Christmas?"

"I'm sorry, but it looks like we'll be spending both holidays in DC this year. There's only two months left until the inauguration and so much work to do before then. But I promise we'll try to get back to New York as often as possible. We're not selling our place here, so this will always be our second home."

"Well that's some good news, at least." Danielle was stunned by Darcy's announcement. When she'd made the call to Connie, she'd had no idea that the result would be this complete upheaval of Darcy's life and her own. She wasn't sure whether she'd been too impulsive; maybe she should have left well enough alone, but it was too late now. Trying to fix everything was her greatest attribute but probably her greatest fault. It had gotten her in trouble in the past, and now it had precipitated her sister's move to another city.

"It would be wonderful if you, Alex, and Freddy could come for dinner tonight," Darcy said, trying to pacify her sister and change the subject. "We'll talk all this over with Mark. His enthusiasm is contagious. You'll end up helping us pack our bags and throwing us out," she joked. "And I suppose it will be our last family meal together for a while."

"Sure, of course. We'll be there. But I'd better get to work now." Danielle was practically pushing her twin sister out the door. She knew she was about to come unraveled. She could feel the familiar signs of a panic attack beginning. She hadn't experienced one in years. Maybe she'd have to see Dr. Smith again professionally to help her through losing Darcy once again. Quickly looking away, she went over to the sink and began rinsing out her coffee cup so her sister wouldn't see the tears streaming down her cheeks.

"We'll see you at six thirty sharp if that's okay with you, and I'll bring dessert." Danielle hoped her voice sounded normal, because she certainly didn't feel that way ... not at all. And, as had happened in the past, this totally unnecessary physical separation from Darcy was all her fault ... again.

CHAPTER 19

Mark and Mr. Robinson

Mark called their lawyer. "Bill, it's Mark Donavan. I know it's only been a few days, but have you had any luck tracking down the person who made the false allegations about me?"

"No. As I told you before, that will take some time. I've hired an excellent private investigator, and he's working on your case, but he'll need to interview dozens of people. The minute he finds anything of interest, he'll call me.

"Since your dismissal, have you or Darcy thought of anyone who might have a reason to hurt you? Anyone you innocently harmed or someone who's very jealous of your success, personal or professional?"

"We can't think of a single person," Mark reiterated. "And we've talked about it endlessly."

"I've been thinking," Mr. Robinson continued. "I think it's odd that someone you barely know was the person who fired you. Why not your immediate boss? That would be the normal procedure. There must have been a reason."

Mark hadn't thought of that before, but Mr. Robinson was correct. It was strange. "I'm also calling because Darcy and I have some good news of our own," he said. "We are leaving New York this weekend. We've taken jobs in the Pierce administration, so we're moving back to DC. I know I will need a security background check. Can you possibly suppress my dismissal, since no public allegations were made by the network? I'm sure I can't work at the White House without a top-secret clearance." He was worried. "You have our old address in your files. And," he said, emphasizing his words, "whatever it costs, I want to know who did this to us. Who hated me so much to want to ruin my career?"

"I understand. Trust me, Mark. I'll take care of the top-secret business right away and will be in touch," Mr. Robinson assured his client. "Don't worry. Give Darcy my best, and congratulations to both of you on your new jobs. They certainly came along at just the right time." He hung up but couldn't help but wonder whether the timing of the new positions was purely coincidental.

CHAPTER 20

The Whole Gang

Darcy and Mark and Alex and Danielle sat in the Donavans' spacious living room, chatting and watching Freddy play with his toys. Darcy always kept a chest full of them for Freddy and constantly added new ones. She and Mark loved to spoil their nephew.

"This news of yours is so exciting." Alex grinned. "Nathan is a lucky man to have you two by his side. I remember when he was running for senator from Massachusetts. Danielle and I volunteered and worked on his campaign. He is so honorable, and the experience was very gratifying. Connie and Nathan are delightful people, and hopefully you'll get to know their son, Frank, and his wife too. They are a sweet young couple who live somewhere in the metropolitan DC area."

"I agree with my husband." Danielle smiled warmly. "This is exciting for you and great for our country." She'd had time after her successful interview with Don March earlier to really think about and appreciate what a truly miraculous opportunity Nathan and Connie had given Darcy and Mark. And she decided not to tell them about the small part she'd played in it. "I have to admit, I'm a little jealous. You are going to be surrounded by powerful and interesting people, while I will be surrounded by dirty diapers and formula bottles. You have to promise to keep a journal so you can write another book when you finish the job."

In all the rush and confusion surrounding the move, Darcy hadn't given the idea of starting another book any thought. But now that

Danielle mentioned it, she agreed it was a great idea. She'd already published two best sellers in the past and still had her agent and established contacts in the publishing world. "I suppose I'll have to sign some sort of a nondisclosure form at the White House, but I bet I can find enough juicy gossip and fun facts not prohibited by that agreement to fill a new book … maybe not a historically accurate biography but a scintillating novel perhaps. Thanks for the suggestion." She winked at her sister. "Maybe you'll cowrite it with me someday."

Danielle was an excellent writer, and Darcy would welcome her input and expertise if the book really did materialize. Time would tell.

They all enjoyed dinner together, topped off with an ice cream cake Danielle had bought for this special family dinner. It was Freddy and Mark's favorite flavor … chocolate with red and white sprinkles on the icing. After the meal, Danielle put Freddy to bed in the guest room, and the adults continued their conversation.

"I think we've made all the necessary arrangements for our condo here." Mark seemed pleased. "I've canceled the newspapers and given the mailman our change of address."

"And I have the suitcases laid out, so tomorrow I'll decide what to take. We left lots of clothes in the DC apartment, so we don't have to pack much. We even have winter coats there."

"I can always send anything you forgot," Danielle offered. "I'm going to miss you two so much!" She looked at Darcy and Mark and couldn't help herself. She started to cry.

"There's always Facetime," Alex reminded his wife gently. "With that we can keep in touch, and Freddy can talk to Darcy and see her all the time. Darcy and Mark can see baby Caroline the minute she arrives in this world and every day thereafter. It's the best we can do under the circumstances. Thank God for modern technology."

"Okay," Danielle reluctantly agreed, "I was just being selfish." She looked at Alex and grinned. "With all this White House news, I forgot to tell you mine. Today I hired an old medical school friend of Alex's to be Healing Words' new executive director. That means I'll be able to work from home most days and will have more free time. We can come visit you in Washington whenever I can drag Alex out of the hospital.

Poor baby has been working extra hard this semester. Look at him." She nodded lovingly toward her husband. "Poor guy's so exhausted that he's about to fall asleep at the table."

"I am not," Alex protested, but he had to admit to himself that he was very tired and struggling to stay awake. It was barely nine o'clock. His extraordinary fatigue seemed to be happening more and more lately, and he used it as an excuse to avoid the gym. He knew he was out of shape but couldn't find the time to work out anymore. He was mildly concerned about his health and planned to schedule a physical when he could find the time.

"But seriously, with a toddler and a new baby, I'm not sure how much free time you're really going to have." Mark looked concerned as he spoke to Danielle. "Have you considered hiring a full-time nanny? I know you've made do so far with babysitters, but now you'll need another pair of hands around the house pretty permanently."

"That's on my to-do list." Danielle smiled. "I'll start to look around. I know I can't have two kids at home and work from here effectively without some backup help."

They continued talking for another hour. Then Alex went into the guest bedroom, picked up his sleeping son, and led his family back downstairs to their own apartment. Darcy and Mark washed the glasses and dishes, put away Freddy's toys, and sat by the fireplace for a night cap before turning in.

"I guess that's our last family dinner together for quite a while," Darcy said sadly, fighting the tears she felt forming in her eyes. "I will miss them."

"You never know." Mark tried to cheer her up. "We'll have to skip Thanksgiving and Christmas here this year, but maybe we can sneak back into town for a day or two somewhere during the holidays ... maybe for New Year's."

"I hope so." Darcy cuddled up to Mark. "After everything Danielle and I did to reconcile after our long estrangement, I don't want anything to separate us ever again. I never want to lose our special connection."

"You won't," he promised her. "Not ever again. Neither one of you would allow that to happen."

"By the way, did you notice how tired Alex seemed?" Darcy said. "I think Danielle's right. He's working too hard, and his color is a little off."

"Yes, I noticed," Mark responded. "I'll talk to him tomorrow about slowing down a bit and maybe getting a checkup. In the meantime, I could use a good night's sleep myself. Care to join me in the boudoir, Mrs. Donavan?"

She smiled and said, "I thought you'd never ask."

Part 2

CHAPTER 21

Darcy

Darcy and Mark arrived in Washington, DC, on the Saturday before Thanksgiving. They unpacked their clothes and personal belonging, and settled into their old condo, soon feeling right at home. The apartment had been cleaned by the Merry Maids, and the refrigerator and pantry were filled with food thanks to online grocery shopping.

It felt strange, however, not having Danielle, Alex, and Freddy living close by in the same building. They could never be replaced, but over time Darcy and Mark hoped to fill that void by reconnecting with their many friends and former business colleagues in town. On Sunday, they slept late and relaxed in their pajamas all day long. In the afternoon they watched the Redskins win their game against the Eagles. The game was perfect for their first full day back in Washington and the last restful one they would have for many weeks.

Early the next morning, they drove to the Pierces' home, located in the prestigious Kalorama neighborhood of northwest DC. There they spent tedious hours filling out mounds of paperwork and applying for security clearances, White House badges, and anything else the bureaucratic government officials required of them. It was not an exhilarating first day on the job.

At five thirty they happily left the odious paperwork behind and joined Connie and Nathan in their library for a cocktail and for their first chance to talk privately with the presidential couple.

"I am so happy to have you here, Darcy." Connie hugged Darcy warmly and handed her a glass of California chardonnay. "I'm a bit overwhelmed by all I'm expected to do as First Lady. I really need your organizational skills, and I'll be needing your advice on just about everything, including confidentially on how to keep Ginger from sticking her nose in places where it doesn't belong." She sighed deeply. Her relationship with her sister-in-law had always been a challenge.

"You flatter me, Connie, but I'll accept the compliment. However, everyone knows you did a fabulous job as the wife of our handsome senator from Massachusetts." She winked at Nathan. "If you survived the demands of that job, this position will be just a little bit harder."

"From your lips to God's ears." Connie grinned at her friend. "Let's get some business over with, and then we can all relax." She pulled out some notes. "Beginning tomorrow, I'd like to set up regular meetings with you every morning at 8:00 a.m. here at the house. Unfortunately, that will mean even on Thanksgiving and Christmas day too. We simply have too much to do to take time off for the holidays this year. I hope that's acceptable. I know you always spend them with Danielle and her family."

"Yes. It's okay. I expected as much this year and have already warned my sister that we'd have to settle for holiday facetime this year. I'm ready to hit the ground running."

"Good. Tomorrow we'll meet with the joint congressional committee on inaugural ceremonies. That group will get you up to speed about what's been decided so far and what to expect. They'll explain all the particulars about the swearing-in ceremony, Nathan taking the oath of office, and the luncheon to follow in the National Statuary Hall of the US Capitol.

"That luncheon is quite a detailed event, which includes the meal, speeches, gift presentations from Congress to Nathan and his vice president, and toasts to the new administration. Then we have to walk or ride down Pennsylvania Avenue to the White House, leading a procession of ceremonial military regiments, citizens' groups, marching bands, and floats. Nathan and I; the vice president, Jennifer Perez, and her husband, Luis; and special guests, including you and Mark, will sit in the reviewing stands as the parade passes by. I wish Danielle and Alex could be there with us, but I am certain her obstetrician doesn't want her to travel so near her due date."

"Yes, she's very disappointed," Darcy added. "But little Mis Caroline comes first now. However, there's always your second term."

Connie moved her hands into a praying position and continued. "Thankfully our transition team doesn't have to organize the parade. That's handled by the joint task force. The parade, as you know, is a much-anticipated event for millions of Americans watching from the streets here and across the country on television. We want everything to go off with precision."

"Wow, I'm tired just thinking about that day." Darcy laughed. But no challenge was too massive for her to tackle. It was one of the reasons Connie had selected her for this job. "And that's just before the balls start."

Connie rolled her eyes. "It's a lot to do in twelve hours. Historically, the swearing-in begins precisely at noon on January twentieth, and then the balls will last well into the wee morning hours … a long, long day followed by a much longer night."

"But when will we actually move your things into the White House?" Darcy was curious about the timetable and the logistics. If she was to be in charge, she wanted everything to come off seamlessly to reflect well on the first family.

"You and I will make all the arrangements for that during these next two months. We'll select what furniture we want and decide exactly where it's to go. The actual move will take place during the swearing-in ceremonies and during the afternoon's activities. Teams of professionals will move the former president out and us into the White House simultaneously. It should take about six hours, if we've organized everything properly. It's like a major change of scenery on the stage of a Broadway show.

"When it comes time for us to dress for the balls, everything should be hanging in our closets and all our clothes put away in our drawers. Even our personal photos will have been placed where we've noted, and our computers should be up and running in the private residence, the East and West Wings and the Oval Office. It requires superb organization and probably a little luck."

"What's the first thing you need me to do?" Darcy asked, feeling a little overwhelmed.

"It may sound silly in light of everything we have to plan ... but organizing my wardrobe is imperative. I don't have time to shop, so I'll need you to arrange for an adequate set of outfits to carry me through the first couple of weeks, and then I'll find a personal shopper.

"One of our many dedicated volunteers has arranged for several prominent American designers to present their wardrobe suggestions to me this week. I'll need to pick out appropriate outfits to wear at all those inaugural functions and make a dress plan going forward that can guide my personal shoppers. I'm told that I need to establish guidelines and preferences, favorite fabrics, styles, etcetera. When I say 'I,' I mean 'we.' I can't do this without your help and input."

Connie continued, "I want the American public to like what I wear. I hope they will be proud of how I look because I represent them, but I'm not a fashion freak, as you know. I prefer tailored, classic clothes, muted colors with scarves or hats to accessorize and add a bit of color. I really don't have a signature style. I've never had the time to develop one or frankly the interest. I am not a Nancy Reagan or Jackie Kennedy."

"Well, that's going to change. We'll figure out a signature style together," Darcy reassured her friend. "Let's see what the designers come up with, and then I'll contact some personal shoppers I know from Saks, Bloomingdales, and Neiman Marcus. By the end of next week, we'll have you outfitted for all your official appearances, and then we can concentrate on building a complete wardrobe for all other occasions. One step at a time."

"Sounds good," Connie said with relief. "I knew I could count on you to take charge. Now let's enjoy our wine and join the men. The rest can wait until tomorrow."

* * *

Mark and Nathan leaned against the library's mahogany bar, enjoying their cocktails, and watched Connie and Darcy. "Those two get along great," Nathan remarked affectionately. "Connie made a great decision in selecting your wife to help her. I think she should change her title from personal assistant to chief of staff."

"Darcy doesn't care about a title. She couldn't be more thrilled to be working for Connie, and she won't disappoint her. I've never seen anyone as organized, and she never runs out of ideas or energy. I hope I won't disappoint you either. Other than the obvious, tell me what you expect from me and how you envision us interacting once you're living in the White House."

"Well, I've studied past administrations," Nathan began. "Their press secretaries held daily briefings with the media and the White House correspondents. In this age of twenty-four-hour news, that may not be necessary. I was thinking three officially scheduled briefings a week should be sufficient, unless something urgent comes up that needs our immediate attention. Your primary responsibility will be as the official spokesperson for the administration. You will be excellent because you have the perfect broadcasting skill set. Explaining political decisions and situations to the press is much the same as broadcasting a sporting event to the public. In many ways, politics is the same thing as sports ... a long game with the outcome hoped for but unknown. It's constant sparring between the White House and the reporters, but you must always be honest and present the administration's point of view. That means that even if you disagree with me, you may tell me in private but never voice that opinion in public.

"I want you to sit in on almost all my meetings so you will fully understand my positions and be able to articulate them accurately ... thus the need for your top-security clearance. You will know almost everything I do and be my public voice and my personal sounding board.

"As the keystone piece of my administration, I plan to concentrate on cleaning up the environment and boosting and rebuilding our nation's infrastructure. Our airports are a disgrace. Our mass transportation is a joke. The systems in Europe and elsewhere put ours to shame."

"I feel your passion." Mark laughed at his friend. "You sound like you're making your State of the Union address, not chatting with a friend over an excellent scotch."

"My apologies. You got me there." Nathan looked embarrassed and chuckled. "I get so excited about all the possibilities of what we can do for this country that I tend to get carried away. Sometimes in bed at night, I get so worked up that poor Connie has to shove a pillow over my face to get me to stop talking."

"Well, I won't do that," Mark assured him. "I'll leave that to your wife. You can ramble on and on with me anytime. How about we join the girls now and relax a bit?"

CHAPTER 22

Danielle

Danielle threw herself into work, helping Don March get settled in at Healing Words and teaching him everything she could about the program and how it worked. She spent hour upon hour with him, and they began to forge a strong, respectful friendship. She had been so wrong about her first impression of him. He wasn't arrogant or rude. He was simply a strong-minded man with independent thoughts. Sometimes they agreed, and sometimes they were like oil and water, but so far, they had managed to compromise. Danielle enjoyed going to work in large part because of her interactions with Don, and she thrived on being part of the new innovations he instituted.

She missed her twin sister terribly, and there wasn't a morning when she didn't have a short cry. She often tried to call, but Darcy was always too busy to talk. Darcy sent Danielle short texts, explaining what she and Mark were doing and how things in DC were progressing, but she didn't have time for their normal, lengthy sisterly talks or even to Facetime with little Freddy. Darcy's new job was absorbing all her time and energy, but she seemed to be thriving.

Danielle had called Dr. Smith in Boston every day of the first week Darcy was gone. She needed to express her sorrow at the separation and admit that Darcy's move was partially her fault for reaching out to Connie. Having been her therapist in Boston for a considerable time, Dr. Smith knew all about the twins' histories and interdependence on each other. He tried to reassure Danielle that she had done a loving thing by asking Connie to look into possible jobs for Darcy and Mark. The result was wonderful for them but not what Danielle had anticipated. The unexpected separation had left Danielle feeling less than whole and on shaky emotional ground.

Dr. Smith knew Danielle could function independently from Darcy. She had for the fifteen years they were estranged. However, his words of encouragement lasted only about twenty-four hours before Danielle felt anxious and insecure again, and called him back. He didn't mind. He adored her as both a former patient and now a colleague and friend, but he was beginning to think he might need to refer her to a psychiatrist in New York for extra moral support. He didn't feel comfortable treating her now that they were so close personally and working together at Healing Words. He was sure once the new baby came, Danielle would be too busy to worry about Darcy's departure, but that was still weeks away.

Alex missed Darcy and Mark too, but he wasn't as undone by their move to DC as Danielle. He also tried to reassure Danielle and even called Dr. Smith for advice about how to help his wife with her perceived loss. Ray Smith knew about the twins' unique relationship and explained that Danielle's pregnancy hormones were running wild. She wasn't having a breakdown or any kind of relapse, as Alex feared. She was simply exhausted because the baby kicked and moved around all night. Danielle hadn't had a good night's sleep in several months and was still suffering from morning sickness.

"To put it delicately," Dr. Smith gently kidded Alex, "your wife's a hormonal mess, but the situation will straighten itself out once the baby comes and Danielle's body returns to normal. Darcy's sudden move to DC hasn't helped the situation. The timing is unfortunate, but it's not responsible for Danielle's recent tailspin. Her pregnancy is totally to blame."

After his talk with Dr. Smith, Alex felt better. At least there was an end in sight regarding Danielle's suffering.

"Hi, sweetheart," Alex called out as he patted Hippocrates on the head and came into the kitchen. "Are you having a better day?" He hated to ask that because sometimes the question itself set Danielle off.

However, he was pleasantly surprised when she kissed him warmly and passed him a drink and a plate of cheese and crackers.

"Today was much better," she answered honestly. "I think with Ray's help I'm finally coming to terms with all the changes that have happened in the last month or so ... Don March's arrival and Darcy's departure. As much as I like Don now, it's been very hard for me to accept the fact that he will be taking over my program. I realize that I've said I wanted to step back and spend more time with our family, but saying it and doing it are two different things."

Alex understood completely. It had been very difficult for him to walk away from surgery, but his change of jobs had been brought on by his physical limitations. "Don's a terrific man, and I know he doesn't want to push you out. He's said as much to me many times. He simply wants to help. He's grateful for everything you've done to establish and run Healing Words, and he wants to add his own spin to the program and guide its growth."

"I know that intellectually, but my emotions sometimes get the best of me. I've been spending a lot of time with him, and I like him better and better. This will all work out in time. Don't worry. I'm not falling apart. I promise you." She shot him a hopeful glance.

"I know, honey. But you've been under a lot of stress. Are you feeling any better about Darcy's move?" Even with Dr. Smith's reassurance, he still harbored the thought that his wife might suffer a relapse or have another breakdown if she was under too much pressure.

"I can't deny that I am sad. I hope once the inauguration is over, things will settle down, and we can at least have long phone calls, and Freddy can Facetime them. He misses them too. And I can't wait for baby Caroline's arrival. I am so tired of feeling sick and being so fat. Promise me ... no more babies after her. I can't take another pregnancy."

"You have my solemn promise." He hugged her tightly. "I adore you, Danielle, and I swear on my mother's grave that I can't stand another of your pregnancies either. This one has really worn me out. I can't remember ever being so tired."

She glanced at him to see whether he was kidding. He looked serious though, and for the first time she noticed dark circles under his eyes.

Apparently, she'd been too preoccupied to notice that she wasn't the only one having difficulty sleeping. Alex looked exhausted, and his normally brilliant eyes were clouded and dull.

"Let's go to bed," she suggested lovingly. "We both need to sleep."

He took her by the hand and led her to the bedroom. In spite of her huge belly, he wanted to hold her and make love, but he was too tired and fell asleep the minute his head hit the pillow.

CHAPTER 23

Darcy

Darcy stared out her living room window. The condo's driveway and Massachusetts Avenue were covered with a light dusting of new snow. The trees and bushes lining the property glistened brilliantly in the bright sunlight. It was a beautiful day in Washington for Nathan Pierce and his vice president, Jennifer Perez, to take their oaths of office.

All the hours of planning and coordinating were about to pay off. At exactly noon, Nathan would be sworn in as president of the United States, while his and Connie's clothes and personal belongings would be moved and put in place in the private living quarters at the White House. She and Connie had organized this transition down to the smallest detail. The Pierces' favorite toothpaste and shampoos would be in their bathroom, and their family pictures would be placed all around the residence. The refrigerator would be stocked with lemonade and Diet Coke for Nathan and diet iced tea and fat-free yogurts for Connie. Bowls of Tootsie Rolls would be everywhere. Nathan's tuxedo and Connie's ball gown—and a spare of each, just in case—would be carefully laid out on their bed with all the necessary accessories, shoes, and even their underwear. Darcy had left nothing to chance. She had filled an entire spiral notebook with details about the move-in alone.

"Are you almost ready?" Mark called to her from their bedroom. "We need to leave in a couple of minutes."

"Yes, I think so." She picked up her clipboard and reviewed it one more time, checking off a few more items. "I think I've got everything covered. I can't wait to get this day started."

"Okay then. Let's go." He strolled casually into the room and saw Darcy silhouetted against the window. He stood there, awestruck for a minute, admiring how stunning she was in her midnight-blue, long-sleeved Dior wool dress and matching fitted overcoat. The outfit accentuated her beautiful figure and showed off her gorgeous legs. She wore ankle-length soft suede boots in the same blue. Her long, blonde hair was clipped into a soft twist, and she wore gold dangle earrings he had given her for Christmas. It was Connie's day, but Darcy would inadvertently steal the spotlight and make all the fashion magazines, although that thought had never crossed her mind. To her this day was all about making their dear friends, Nathan and Connie, proud and ensuring that everything went smoothly and according to plan.

Darcy and Mark rode together silently to the Capitol, each lost in his or her own thoughts and feeling a bit overwhelmed by the pomp and circumstance and importance of what was about to happen to them and their country. They were scheduled to meet the rest of Connie and Nathan's family and their invited guests on the Capitol steps and enter the swearing-in ceremony together.

The Pierces' only son, Frank, and his wife, Amy, would be there, proudly supporting his father's success. Nathan's indominable sister, Ginger Gardner, and her husband, Lloyd, would also be front and center, with Ginger claiming sole credit for his election. This was the moment Ginger had dreamed about … her baby brother becoming president of the United States and she being by his side. She called herself the "First Sister," although there was no such official designation.

Ginger and Darcy had a long, personal history together, and they loved each other profoundly. Many years ago, Ginger had almost become her mother-in-law. Her only son, Jason, had been engaged to Darcy when the two were young and just out of college, but they had eventually broken off the engagement and gone their separate ways as friends. Jason later married his friend, Edward, a wonderfully cultured older gentleman. Ginger had trouble accepting her son's sexual orientation and never came to terms with it until after his tragic death in a fiery airplane crash. Darcy had been instrumental in helping Ginger cope with and accept her son's homosexual life style and in welcoming Edward into her family.

By then Darcy had fallen madly in love with Mark Donavan and moved to New York City to work with him in sports broadcasting. Now after so many years, Ginger was thrilled that Nathan and Connie had convinced Darcy and Mark to return to DC and her life again. She loved Darcy like a daughter and was looking forward to spending time with her. Except for the tragic loss of her only son, Ginger's life had never been happier.

The black government limousine pulled slowly up to the Capitol steps. It was eleven thirty. Darcy grabbed Mark's hand and squeezed it tightly as they made their way up the stairs and into the anteroom where they were to meet the others. They were a half hour away from witnessing history.

CHAPTER 24

Danielle

Danielle woke from her nap with a start when she heard Freddy and Alex returning to the apartment. They were laughing and obviously had enjoyed a wonderful time together.

"Hi, Hipps." Freddy patted the statue affectionately and put his mittens on the tray the sculpture held. He couldn't correctly pronounce the name Hippocrates no matter how many times Danielle and Alex made him practice saying it. It always came out as "Hipps."

"Hi, guys," Danielle said as she wandered out of the bedroom. "Did you have a good time at the park?" She warmly embraced them both.

"Yes." Freddy squealed with delight as he jumped up and down and ran around the room, arms spread wide, pretending to be an airplane.

"Is he on a sugar high?" she asked Alex in alarm, recognizing the symptoms. Alex was always too lenient with his son and fed him cookies and candy all the time.

"Maybe a little," her husband answered sheepishly. "We did have a few snacks on our outing... some cotton candy and Cracker Jacks at the zoo and then some ice cream in the park."

"Men." Danielle rolled her eyes. "Now I'll never get him down for his nap."

"The nap can wait," Alex replied with a grin. "I promised our little man that he could watch TV and see Aunt Darcy and Uncle Mark.

Freddy's super excited. He said it will be way better than Facetiming them."

Danielle looked at her watch. "It's getting close to the time. Why don't you put on your sweatpants and slippers so you'll be more comfortable, and I'll turn on the TV." She went over to their flat-screen TV and reached for the remote. "What channel?"

"The inauguration will be on every one, I'd imagine. Turn on CNN or FOX, and we can switch back and forth. I'll get changed and be right back. By the way, for an old pregnant broad, you look mighty sexy." He winked.

She laughed and self-consciously pulled her "Pierce for President" sweatshirt down to hide her basketball stomach, but it was futile. She was much too big. Nothing could disguise her baby bulge.

The three of them took their seats on the sofa and watched in fascination as a procession of dignitaries, congressmen and congresswomen, senators, past presidents, and distinguished guests were led to their seats in anticipation of the arrival of President-Elect Nathan Pierce and his wife, Connie; and Vice President-Elect Jennifer Perez and her husband, Luis.

"Look," Danielle announced proudly. "See. There's Aunt Darcy and Uncle Mark."

Freddy's eyes grew big, and he was glued to the set. When he recognized his aunt and uncle walking to their seats, he smiled broadly and blew a kiss toward the television set. "Aunt Darcy's soooo pretty."

"Yes. She is indeed," Danielle answered wistfully, looking at herself in pajamas while twenty pounds overweight. "She looks gorgeous, and Uncle Mark cleaned himself up pretty well too. Now, quiet please. I want to hear what the commentators are saying."

The cameras focused on Darcy and Mark, and the commentator told the audience they were Mrs. Pierce's personal assistant, Darcy Donavan, and President-Elect Pierce's press secretary, Mark Donavan. Then the Pierces' son, Frank, and his pretty new wife were seated. The announcer next pointed out the arrival of Ginger and Lloyd Gardner, the president-elect's sister and brother-in-law. That completed the family section.

The cameras panned the audience of invited guests but kept returning to focus on Darcy. She was far and away the most attractive and beautifully dressed woman on the podium, and the camera loved her.

"This is unbelievably exciting." Danielle choked up. "I can't believe what we're watching. What a great day this is for our country. I wish Freddy was old enough to remember this. Did you remember to tape this?" she asked her husband. "We have to have a permanent record."

He patted her hand and nodded.

Alex hugged her tightly and whispered, "Honey, if you'd been able to travel, the cameras would be on you the whole time." He knew she was feeling sad and left out because her pregnancy had kept her from attending the inauguration ceremonies. She was so fond of Connie and Nathan and would have done just about anything to share this special moment with them, but she couldn't go against her doctor's advice and endanger her unborn child. If Nathan won a second term, she would move heaven and earth to be there.

The cameras focused on the top of the stairway as the Pierces and the Perezes came into view. The four of them started walking happily down the stairs, stopping to shake hands with the various guests on both sides of the aisles, and finally took their seats in the front row.

Tradition dictated that the vice president be sworn in first to set the stage for the presential oath. Jennifer Perez proudly took her vows with her husband, Luis, at her side.

At precisely noon, Nathan stood up with his right hand raised and his left hand on the Pierces' family Bible; his wife, Connie, stood proudly by his side.

The chief justice of the Supreme Court administered the oath.

"I swear that I will faithfully execute the office of president of the United States and will, to the best of my ability, preserve, protect, and defend the Constitution of the United States, so help me God." Nathan proudly spoke the words loudly and kissed his wife. The crowd burst into tumultuous applause.

A military band played a stirring rendition of "Hail to the Chief," which was followed by the traditional twenty-one-gun salute and thunderous applause.

Nathan stood at the podium, overlooking the tens of thousands of people who had come to Washington to witness and celebrate this moment. He made a stirring and memorable address, which was interrupted numerous times by more appreciative shouts of support and applause.

At the end of the ceremony, the new president and vice president led their invited guests up the stairs and into Statuary Hall of the Capitol, where they would attend the congressional luncheon before viewing the inaugural parade.

"That was spectacular." Danielle hugged Freddy. "What a wonderful day! You should be very proud of your aunt and uncle. They will be a part of history now and forever."

"Yes, it was beyond wonderful," Alex agreed. "I am so proud of Connie and Nathan—and Darcy and Mark, of course. I feel good things are about to happen for our country and the whole world." The inauguration had deeply moved him.

"Nathan's speech was fabulous, and Connie looked wonderful. I recognized Darcy's taste in the red outfit she selected for our new First Lady to wear. It set precisely the right understated, elegant, patriotic tone." Danielle loved Darcy's taste in clothes and tried to emulate it. As kids, the twins had always dressed alike, but Darcy always chose the outfits.

Danielle put Freddy on the floor to play with a puzzle and looked over at Alex. Are you feeling okay?" she asked with concern when she noticed his ankles were very swollen.

"I'm just fine," Alex answered a little too quickly. "Just tired, I guess, and completely overwhelmed by what we just witnessed. How about we order a pizza to celebrate?"

"Sure," Danielle answered warily. As a doctor and his wife, she didn't like that Alex appeared to be retaining fluids. Swollen ankles could portend a lot of conditions … none of which were good. She didn't want to ruin today's celebration, but tomorrow she would insist that he see a doctor for a thorough checkup.

CHAPTER 25

Darcy and Mark were seated at a table with Frank and Amy Pierce, Ginger and Lloyd Gardner, and two supreme court justices and their wives. Unobtrusively Darcy pulled her phone out of her purse and checked her messages. There were none, so she sent a text to George Harris, the man in charge of the Pierces' move into their quarters at the White House. She asked whether there were any problems and whether everything would be completed by the end of the parade.

"Everything's going according to plan, and we'll be done early, no later than 5:00 p.m. Don't worry, Darcy. Have a good time," George Harris replied. Everyone involved with the move-in appreciated how hard Darcy had worked to ensure a smooth transition.

She sighed with relief and lifted her champagne glass to join in the toasts to the new president and vice president. She looked over at Ginger, who was beaming from ear to ear. "So far everything is perfect," she mouthed, and Ginger nodded happily.

"I need to talk to you when this is over," Ginger mouthed back.

The luncheon began with opening remarks from Senator Chuck Schumer. He was followed by the Reverend Jorge Sinsa, the vice president's pastor, who gave the invocation.

The presidential head table and all the distinguished guests in the room dined on New England clam chowder and steamed lobster for their first course. The second course was grilled cedar plank salmon or filet mignon with wild huckleberry reduction, butternut squash puree, golden beets, or green beans. There were then more toasts, and finally the president and vice president were presented with hand-cut Lenox crystal bowls with etchings of the Capitol, the White House, and the Washington Monument.

As apple pie with vanilla ice cream and aged cheddar cheese were served, Nathan made a few remarks and thanked the joint congressional committee for the delicious lunch. "I hope all my dealings with Congress will be as satisfying as this meal," he joked.

After the benediction, the guests seated at the official head table made their exits, and the rest of the crowd stayed to mingle, awaiting their instructions to leave. Ginger urgently pulled Darcy aside.

"I have the most amazing news to share with you. I've bitten my tongue so many times in the last few weeks since the election, because I didn't want to say or do anything to distract from Nathan's achievements."

That's a first, Darcy thought affectionately. Ginger always wanted the attention.

"But now that my brother is truly our commander and chief, and anything I do or say won't affect his candidacy, I want to tell you that at my ripe old age, I'm going to finally become a grandmother."

Darcy gasped. "But how is that possible? To put it delicately, Jason's dead."

"Yes. Of course, he is, dear. We all know that, but Edward's told me the most exciting and wonderful news."

Darcy continued to look at Ginger, aghast. Had the woman finally lost her mind? Grief did that to some people. Had the death of her only son finally undone her mentally?

"I know this seems impossible," Ginger explained, understanding Darcy's concern. "But before my beloved Jason died in that horrible plane crash, he and Edward had often discussed wanting a family. They were very serious about it and went to one of those places that arranges for surrogate mothers to carry babies."

Darcy sat back down at the table in shock. "Wait a minute." She choked out the words. "Jason died over six years ago. How could he be the father of this supposed grandchild of yours? I'm sorry to burst your bubble, but I think you're being scammed, Ginger. Someone's trying to take advantage of your vulnerability."

"No, no. It's perfectly legitimate. Edward explained everything to me and showed me all the paperwork from the center where they froze Jason's sperm for his future use. The place is called New Hope, and it's supposed to be the leading surrogacy and egg donation center in the United States. It's been in business for over twenty years and has a sterling reputation. Believe me, Lloyd had the place thoroughly checked out.

"Naturally," Ginger continued, "my son had no idea he'd be dead in a few months. He and Edward felt they had plenty of time and had planned to start the insemination process within the year. After Jason's death, Edward was in such a state of shock that he completely forgot all about it. It wasn't until he received a bill a few months ago for the cost of continued refrigeration of the sperm that he remembered Jason's wish to have a child. And so, after careful thought, he honored that commitment. As Jason's husband, he gave permission for the insemination. Apparently, my son's sperm were still viable, and his baby will be born in six months, by the middle of July."

"I can't believe this." Darcy was incredulous. "I didn't know such things were possible. You're really telling me that Jason's child will be born this summer and that you and Lloyd and Edward are all right with it and plan to raise the baby together?"

"Yes, dear. That's exactly what I'm telling you. I know this is a shock, but can you please be happy for me, for all of us? In death Jason has given me the greatest gift."

Darcy was too stunned to answer. She just stared wide eyed at Ginger. This was so bizarre. She had no idea what Ginger expected her to say.

"As you know, I wasn't a very good mother to Jason. I overindulged him and never held him accountable for his often-childish behavior. I always hoped you'd marry him, help him mature, and become the mother of my grandchildren. That wasn't in the cards for lots of reasons, as you know, but now Lloyd and I have a second chance to make up for our past mistakes. I know all three of us are considered old people, but between us, we have a lot of wisdom and love to give this child. What do you think?"

Darcy was too stunned to answer. She could see only problems ahead.

CHAPTER 26

Danielle

Danielle leaned casually over Don's shoulder to look at the graphs and spreadsheets. "These are quite impressive," she said. "I can't believe how quickly you've added so much more scope and creativity to our materials."

"I like visuals," he replied thoughtfully. "I think they make the point very strongly. Healing Words has been a huge success, but there's room for so much more expansion. The opportunities are almost endless."

"I know," Danielle agreed. "I am just afraid that if the program gets too big, it will lose its personal touch and become just like another self-help book that lies dormant and dusty on someone's shelf and is never read."

"No, never. I don't propose we expand too rapidly … one step at a time. I do, however, have what I think is a great idea. Are you ready?" He hoped she would approve.

She looked at him apprehensively. She wasn't one for surprises. "I don't know. Am I?"

"Yes, I think so." He smiled. "I believe you should make videos of all your previous talks from the program's inception. And going forward, continue to tape each new one. Having that library of actual sessions showing you interacting with the patients will be a great tool for convincing other institutions to accept the program. If other group leaders can use your tapes as a guide, that will decrease the number of actual days you'll have to travel to our other sites and hospitals. It will give you the freedom and flexibility to spend more time at home once the baby arrives ... and I know we are a nonprofit, but you can sell the tapes and put the money back in the company coffers to keep it in the black without touching anymore of your personal funds."

"Wow. What a great idea. That's exactly what I'd like to do. Ideally, one day here in the office each week, one day on site somewhere locally, and the other three days working from home. That's a schedule I can live with, and I can plan my childcare accordingly." Danielle was thrilled.

"Do you know how many minutes a normal session takes?" He had watched her conduct them so many times but never paid attention to their length. Somehow, when he was with her, he lost track of time.

"If no patient is in crisis, the workshops last a little over an hour. If someone is in distress, I usually single him or her out and speak privately with them for as long as it takes. That's unpredictable."

"Understood. If you decide that you want to do this, when would you be available to start the tapings?" He didn't want to push her, but he wanted to capitalize on her enthusiasm. "I'd like to have a few dozen tapes completed before you take your maternity leave. If you agree, I can arrange to get all the necessary equipment together. All I need is you."

He meant that in more ways than she could possibly imagine. His intense attraction to her had started at their first meeting when he had tried so hard to impress her. As each day, week, and month went by, the pull to her became stronger and harder for him to deny. Only his respect for her and his friendship with Alex kept him from telling her how he felt. He knew his feelings for her weren't returned. Danielle was totally devoted and deeply in love with her husband.

"I guess I could start tomorrow," she said quietly. Her schedule was pretty open. "I'll have to go through my records and notes to organize them. Maybe the day after would be better and give me a little more time to prepare. I wish Darcy was here. She could whip all these session notes into shape in only a few hours."

"Well, she isn't here, but I'll be glad to help," he offered.

He enjoyed spending time with Danielle. She was a warm and caring person. The fact that she was gorgeous and funny didn't hurt either. He'd told Alex many times how lucky Alex was to have her as his wife. Don knew his feelings for Danielle were inappropriate, but he kept telling himself that as long as he didn't act on them, everything would be all right ... no harm no foul.

"Do you want to do the taping in the hospital setting or in your home?" he said.

"I hadn't thought about it, but if we're going to have long sessions, maybe my place would be easier. I can keep an eye on Freddy that way, and then Alex can take over when he gets home. By the way," she said in earnest, "I've noticed that he seems more tired than normal lately. I've nagged him to death about getting a checkup, but he keeps poo-pooing the idea and says he's fine. I'm really worried about how hard he's working. His hours are worse than when he was an operating surgeon. Has he said anything to you about not feeling well?"

"No, not a word. I had lunch with him yesterday, and he seemed fine, but now that you mention it, I think he was a little pale. I'm sure it's nothing to worry about. He loves what he's doing, and that's the important thing. It was a hard transition from operating to teaching."

"I guess I worry too much ... hormones probably." She pushed her concern about her husband's health aside and gathered up her things. Then she went back to the room she was now using as her office since Don had become entrenched in hers. A few hours later, when she had compiled the information she'd need for the first five videos, she went back to say good night. "I organized things faster than I had anticipated. I can be ready to start taping by nine tomorrow morning. Can you be at our place then with your video equipment?"

"Sure thing." He smiled warmly at her, noticing how truly lovely she looked, even at six months pregnant. "I'll be there, and I'll bring the donuts."

"Don't you dare." She laughed. "I'm as big as a house already, and I don't need any more calories. I'll give you coffee and a slice of melon. Will that work?"

"Sounds perfect." He looked back down at the paperwork on his desk to distract himself. She was so innocent and breathtakingly beautiful. It was difficult to keep from staring at her. "Absolutely perfect," he said again. "See you in the morning."

CHAPTER 27

Darcy

Darcy and Mark sat in the presidential viewing stands in front of the White House, watching the inaugural parade as it passed by. Darcy was so distracted by the news about Jason's baby that she was restless and couldn't sit still. She couldn't focus on the merriment, the marching bands, or the floats. She kept thinking of Jason and how happy he'd be if he knew his mother's reactions to Edward and their unborn baby.

Darcy's reaction was completely different. She wasn't sure how she felt about her former fiancé's baby being born years after Jason had been laid to rest. The concept was a little ghoulish. Spooky, in fact. Ginger, however, saw nothing wrong with it and was beyond delighted to have the chance to become a major part of her grandchild's life.

Darcy hadn't had a second to talk to Mark. When they left the Capitol, they had been surrounded by the other dignitaries and guests, and now every time she got his attention and wanted to tell him about the baby, someone came up to shake his hand and schmooze. This wasn't the right time anyway. This news needed to be told in private.

"I want to check on what's happening in the residence." She pulled Connie aside and said quietly, "I'm going to slip out the back. Please tell Mark where I've gone. It should only take me an hour or so. I want everything to be perfect for your first night."

"Okay," Connie answered. "Thanks. And by the way, I kept my good jewelry with me for tonight's balls." She reached into her pocketbook and pulled out a cloth roll-up traveling jewelry case. "Do you suppose it's safe for you to take it now and leave it with my other things? The rest of my pieces are in the deposit box at our bank until I can move them to the White House."

"I'm sure it'll be fine. I'll check with the chief steward and leave the jewelry case with him. He can put it in the safe in the residential quarters for you." She moved to the back of the stands and went out the makeshift door. It was a beautiful late afternoon, and she enjoyed the short walk from the stands across the White House front lawn and into Nathan and Connie's new home. She was stopped by four different secret service officers on the way and asked to show her White House identification. She didn't mind at all. Keeping Connie and Nathan safe was a high priority.

When she arrived upstairs, she found a cast of characters busily at work, following her very detailed instructions. They were bustling around the residence, doing their assigned tasks. Maids were ironing sheets, making beds, vacuuming, and fluffing pillows. Handymen were hanging pictures on the walls and moving furniture where the Pierces had requested. Other staff were stocking the kitchen shelves, putting away groceries, and unpacking the Pierces' china and glassware.

The chief butler had laid Nathan's tux and Connie's ball gown on the love seat in the master bedroom. Darcy checked to make sure everything was there: studs, a bow tie, evening shoes for them both, and appropriate underwear. Nathan was going coatless to the balls. Connie was wearing a cashmere stole that matched her dove-gray, floor-length Tom Ford gown. Darcy placed Connie's jewelry case beside her evening gown and pointed it out to the chief steward, who assured her it would be safe.

Darcy checked her notes and carefully inspected Connie's closets and Nathan's. In each, just as she had organized, their clothes were hung by type, style, and color, with their shoes neatly tucked away on racks. Connie's pocketbooks and hats were on the proper shelves, as were Nathan's gloves and scarves. Everything looked perfect, as if the Pierces had lived there forever, just as Darcy had visualized.

She wandered into the bathrooms and checked that all the prescription medicines, cosmetics, makeup, razors, toothbrushes, and combs were neatly arranged. Everything was in its proper place. She wandered throughout the entire residence, checking every detail; and when she was satisfied, she relaxed and took a moment for herself.

She went into the living room of the private quarters. The staff and volunteers had finished their work and left. She was by herself. She sat on one of the two matching chintz sofas Connie had brought down from their home on the Cape and gazed around the room, taking in the scene, reveling in this extraordinary private moment.

Reaching for her cell phone, she scrolled through her photos until she found her father's picture, taken just a few weeks before he died. He looked so happy and was smiling. An unexpected tear escaped and slowly trickled down her face. *Here I am*, she thought. *Daddy, your little Darcy is sitting in the living room of the most powerful man in the world. If you could see me now, I hope you'd be proud. I've come a long way from that young girl you detested for so many years. Thank God we straightened everything out before you passed away, and we came to love each other again. Karin didn't win in the end. Danielle and I both miss you more than you'll ever know.*

She wiped her tears, put the thoughts of her detestable stepmother out of her mind, and stood up to return to the reviewing stands. It had been an extraordinary day, and she felt proud of her part in it.

CHAPTER 28

Danielle

Don and Danielle continued working together almost every morning, filming her videos. They taped and reproduced her lessons one by one, starting with the original one she had written to begin the program. The work made for exhausting but satisfying days. Alex often commented that he had never seen Danielle look happier, and he was proud of the hard work she was doing to produce the tapes.

Danielle and Alex had hired a nanny, Lynn Canny, who came to the apartment every weekday from eight o'clock in the morning until six o'clock at night. Lynn was about the same age as Danielle; she had never married and was a former practical nurse. She got along easily with Danielle and Alex, and was a real asset to the household. She had taken the job as their nanny because she wanted time away from the hospital setting to rethink her future. She wasn't convinced nursing was meant to be her life's work. She was compassionate and competent, and she adored children. Lynn loved the Healing Words program and admired Danielle immensely. She was a perfect fit for the Stone family. She loved Freddy's exuberant personality and was looking forward to taking care of Caroline as soon as she was born.

Having Lynn in the household was a blessing for Danielle. She watched Freddy, did errands for Danielle, and generally made it possible for Danielle and Don to spend the necessary time together to produce the tapes. Their goal was to have twenty-one completed by Caroline's arrival. It was an arduous undertaking but doable.

Don turned out to be a great partner and was always making constructive suggestions about how to improve the old lectures and invent new ones. Danielle trusted his instincts and no longer felt threatened by him. She had come to admire him and planned to implement some of his new ideas as soon as she returned to work, when Caroline was three months old. She was blissfully happy and totally unaware of Don's increasingly passionate feelings for her. Danielle was completely focused on her family and Healing Words.

Alex had recently come to her and confessed why he had been largely absent from their home and was working such long hours. He shared his dream with her about starting a mentoring project at the hospital. He had seen firsthand that the medical students, interns, and residents were often lost and confused, with no one to talk to about their fears and anxieties. They were supposed to be the healers, the people who fixed things, but there was no one to fix them. He wanted to do something to help. Whether the students were in their first, second, or third year of medical school, they were all worried about the same things ... Had they made the right career decision? Had they picked the right specialty suited to their personality and skills? They obsessed about their grades and were consumed with fears about whether they could pass the dreaded medical boards.

Medical school was an exciting but frightening time for these young people. Many saw deaths for the first time. They witnessed terrible pain and suffering. And the hardest lesson was to accept that sometimes no amount of skills they possessed as physicians or combinations of treatments and medicine they could prescribe would cure or save a patient. The hospital experience affected each one in different, individual ways. Alex explained to Danielle that recent statistics showed that the suicide rate among third-year medical students was alarmingly high and that sometime during their medical training years, many of the students had been or were severely depressed.

Alex felt he needed to do something more important for the medical students than hosting his Wednesday night dinners, although he still loved those evenings and found them rewarding. He decided to begin a program where he would mentor students individually, tutor them if necessary, and help them with vocational counseling. The shape and scope of the mentoring program was just beginning to form in his head. He was excited about the endless possibilities and wanted to recruit his fellow physician colleagues to participate. Ideally, he envisioned that one day every medical student would have a senior staff physician as his or her personal mentor throughout his or her entire medical school training, internship, and residency. The first person he asked to be part of the program, to become a mentor, was his friend, Dr. Don March.

Danielle was surprised. Don hadn't said a word to her about Alex's new program or his part in it. However, she was happy for her husband and glad Don had agreed to help him. It seemed like a massive endeavor. She hoped Alex was up to the task.

CHAPTER 29

Darcy

Darcy returned to the viewing stand and took her seat next to Mark.

"How was everything inside?" he asked. "Everything to your specifications?"

"Absolutely. Connie and Nathan will be really pleased. But I'm so tired. Do you think we can skip out now? I've had enough of this parade."

"Sure, if you want to. Are you feeling all right?"

"Yes, I'm fine, just really exhausted. And I want to talk to you about something Ginger told me. I'd like to go home and take a long hot bath and then order Chinese. Are you game?"

"You bet. Let me say goodbye to Nathan, and we'll be on our way. Do you have any interest in sharing that tub with me?" He smiled mischievously and got up to say his goodbyes.

"Maybe we can Facetime Danielle and Alex. I bet she's as big as a house by now," Darcy suggested.

They made their way to the front to say goodbye to Connie and Nathan. A lot of the other guests had already left, including Ginger and Lloyd, so Darcy didn't have a chance to speak to her again about Jason's baby. "We're leaving now," Darcy whispered to Connie. "Everything's shipshape upstairs. I'll see you in the morning."

"Okay but not too early please. I expect we'll be out pretty late."

Darcy was glad she wasn't expected to attend the balls. I'll see you around noon."

Darcy and Mark returned to their condo, and she saw the flashing light on their landline flicking. "Can you check out the message please?" she pleaded. "I have to get out of these boots. My feet are killing me." She walked into their bedroom while he went to listen to the message.

Darcy undressed and filled the bathtub. She added two scoops of lavender bubble bath and slowly slid beneath the inviting water. She was so tired. She almost dosed off until she felt Mark's hands gently caressing her body. He perched on the side of the tub and slowly ran his fingers down the inside of her arm, over her left breast, down her flat belly, and onto her left thigh.

She relaxed and reveled in the physical sensations he was stirring in her body. She reached up and pulled his face closer, giving him a long, deep kiss. He moaned and continued to slide his finger up the other side of her slim body and gently squeezed her right nipple, making deliciously provocative concentrate circles around it. Darcy shivered with pure sensual pleasure. Suddenly Mark stopped and moved his hand back over her right breast. Pushing down on a spot under her nipple, he asked in alarm, "What's this? How long has this lump been here?"

CHAPTER 30

Danielle

Danielle paced around her living room floor. Why wasn't Alex home? Since he'd started his mentorship program, he was always at the hospital. He called Danielle several times a day to check on her and Freddy, but he rarely made it home for dinner anymore and often came in so late that she was sound asleep. Even on New Year's Eve, he had just made it home in time to watch the ball drop at midnight and then had fallen into a deep sleep before she could kiss him to welcome in the next decade.

His explanation was that there was so much work to do to get the program up and running that he had lost track of time. He promised that when things settled down, he'd return to a normal schedule. She hoped it would be soon, before the new baby came, which could be at any time. The doctor said the baby had dropped and was positioned in the birth canal.

After learning about Alex's mentoring program, Danielle had been very understanding. Alex had always been supportive of her work with Healing Words, especially the extra hours she had been spending with Don lately to make and revise the lesson tapes. He thought that since she was so busy with her own project, she wouldn't miss him so much. But he was wrong. No amount of fulfilling work could replace the intimate times she wanted with her husband. Her world revolved around him, and she missed him every minute he wasn't with her.

"I need you now more than ever," she'd cried emotionally a few nights ago. "I feel fat and ugly and so lonely for you. I feel like I'm in this marriage alone. I don't like it."

"Darling, you're being silly. You are beautiful. Just very pregnant and hormonal ... and our marriage has never been stronger. You know I adore you. I just need a little more time to work out all the ins and outs of this mentorship thing. I know it would have been easier if I'd thought of it a year from now, but the horse is out of the barn. I need to see it through. Please stand by me. I promise it won't be for much longer."

"I understand," she said soberly. "I really do. But I can see that you are always exhausted. You hardly sleep, and when you do, you toss and turn. You never have time to take Freddy to the park anymore, and we never go out to dinner with friends. I'm worried about how all this extra stress and work are affecting your health. Frankly you seem subdued and pale to me. I miss the vibrant Alex I married. I want my sexy, energetic husband back."

He reassured her that he felt fine and was actually energized by the new program. It just consumed a lot more of his time than he had expected. He reminded her of when he'd been an operating trauma surgeon in Boston and often never made it home at night because of emergencies. However, he promised that he'd try to come home early enough each night to have supper with Freddy and put him to bed. That promise had lasted only a few days, and then the same pattern began again.

Danielle continued to pace around the living room and glanced at her watch for the tenth time. It was nearly seven thirty, and Freddy was ready for bed. She angrily threw a pillow on the floor in frustration and went into her son's room to read him his bedtime story.

CHAPTER 31

Darcy

Darcy and Mark went directly to her gyn doctor's office the next morning. They didn't have an appointment but vowed to sit in the waiting room until Darcy could be seen. Both of them were terrified about what the breast lump might mean. Darcy had always had annual mammograms, but she had been lax about self-examining herself every month. There was no breast cancer in her family that she knew about, so she hadn't been particularly concerned about it until now.

Neither Mark nor Darcy had slept at all last night, and both were operating on pure adrenaline and fear. They had spent hours searching the internet for whatever information they could find about breast lumps and cancer. The doctor's receptionist came over to them and whispered that the doctor would squeeze Darcy in after the next patient.

"Thank you," Darcy answered gratefully. "Hopefully we are overreacting, but we are so scared."

"I understand. Try to be patient. The doctor will be with you in just a little while."

Mark began to aimlessly leaf through a woman's magazine on the table, but he had no interest in it and couldn't concentrate. Darcy had a hard time sitting still too. Her mind kept going to what-if scenarios.

"I wanted to tell you what Ginger said to me yesterday," Darcy began, trying to think about something else besides the unwanted lump invading her breast. "Apparently when Jason and Edward got together, they decided they wanted to have a child, become a real family. They went to one of those agencies that finds surrogates for people. Jason gave his sperm, and the center froze and stored it. After Jason died, Edward forgot all about the matter until he got a bill for long-past-due storage. When he realized he could still be a father to Jason's child, he decided to go through with the procedure. Now Ginger and Lloyd have agreed to help Edward, and the three of them plan to raise the child together. I think the whole idea is ridiculous and spooky. But it's too late. The baby is due in July."

Mark stared at her incredulously. "My God, I feel sorry for the poor kid. By the time he's a teenager, all three of them will be one hundred or more years old."

"I know. It's absurd. Can you see the three of them trick-or-treating or taking the kid to Disney on all those fast rides? What are they thinking?" Darcy shook her head in disbelief.

"I don't think Edward is thinking rationally at all," Mark answered. "He must have made an emotional, rash decision as some kind of misguided tribute to Jason, and now he's stuck with the consequences."

"I know it's not my place, but I feel as if I should do something to help out. How can those three stooges possibly raise a baby at their ages?"

"Maybe we can offer to take the kid to his or her soccer games or something like that," Mark offered. "That kid will need to be around younger adults, and I know Jason would have loved to have you involved with his child."

"I would like to do that," Darcy said thoughtfully. "You really wouldn't mind? After all, I did love Jason at one time and hoped to have his children. You're not jealous?"

"No, darling. I'm very secure. I am not threatened by a dead man. I know you love me. Why don't you call Edward and sound him out about us helping? I bet he'll be thrilled and relieved. As much as I've disagreed over the years with Hillary Clinton, she was right when she said, 'It takes a village.' We can be part of that village, if that's what you want."

"Yes, I think it is," she answered solemnly. "We haven't seen Edward in a while. Let's plan a dinner together soon once we figure out our schedules and this." She pointed to her chest. "We should invite Ginger and Lloyd too. Then we'll work something out with the 'Three Stooges' and come up with a way to raise this poor child with group love."

In spite of the tension she was under, Darcy laughed. "I love all three of them, and the nickname, the Three Stooges, is perfect, but keep it between us, please. Don't ever let Ginger, Lloyd, or Edward know we call them that. They would die of mortification."

"My lips are sealed." He started to say more when the receptionist motioned to them. "The doctor will see you now."

CHAPTER 32

Danielle

Danielle wasn't a complainer, but she had to vent her anger to someone, and Don happened to be the only one around. "Ever since Alex started his mentoring program, he's been practically living at the hospital. He's never home." Her voice was full of frustration. "Now that the baby is due any minute and I'm already having contractions, you'd think he'd want to be right by my side all the time, but apparently not."

Don tried to pacify her, but he also was worried about how much time Alex's new program was taking away from Danielle and Freddy.

"He's super excited about the tremendous support the faculty had given him for his mentoring ideas. Almost every one of the senior staff has embraced Alex's idea and volunteered to take on a mentee. I am thrilled to be involved myself," Don said evenly. "Try to cut Alex a little slack. It's like he had a baby, and he's enjoying those first few weeks of unprecedented joy."

"That's just the point," Danielle replied in frustration. "I'm the one having a baby, a real one, and Alex doesn't even seem to care anymore. All he talks about these days are his medical students and their problems. Even when he's home, he's not really present. He's often on the phone with them or doing research for them. Then he falls asleep. I hardly see him. And frankly I'm very worried. He looks like a walking zombie, with dark circles under his eyes. I've caught him taking pills to keep awake and pills to sleep. He lives on black coffee and claims that everything's fine and that it's just my hormones that are out of whack. I'm not so sure."

"I know it's been tough on you," Don conceded. He went over to Danielle and put his arm around her. He cared so much about her and wanted her to be happy. He knew she was right to be worried about Alex. He was too, and he was doing everything he could to help her with Healing Words; but Alex needed to do more on the home front. "I'll speak to Alex when he gets home tonight or first thing in the morning. I know he loves you with all his heart, and I'm sure he doesn't realize how this project of his has affected you. Have you told him?"

"Several times, but he doesn't seem to listen." She was trying not to cry and felt disloyal to be criticizing her husband. She blinked to stop the tears from falling.

"Men can be pretty dense." Don tried to be supportive. "Give him a chance. How about you and I get dinner started? I'll ask Lynn to stay a little later tonight and put Freddy to bed. Then I'll hang around to talk to Alex, if that's all right with you."

"More than all right," she answered gratefully. "Sometimes I don't know what I'd do without you or how I ever survived before you came along."

Dan smiled. Her kind words were music to his ears. His feelings for Danielle were growing stronger and more intense every day. It was becoming increasingly difficult to keep them hidden. He wished he could tell her how he felt, but doing so was impossible. She wouldn't be open to his advances, and he would feel disloyal to Alex. He was in a no-win situation.

Danielle pulled one of her casserole dishes out of the freezer and transferred it to the microwave. She was too tired to make dinner from scratch. "What I wouldn't give for a glass of wine." She sighed wistfully. "But Don, go ahead. Pour yourself a drink. You know where everything is." She looked at her watch. "With any luck, Alex will be here before dinner burns."

The meal was ready in an hour, but Alex still hadn't come home or called. Don, Danielle, Freddy, and Lynn ate quietly together at the kitchen table, making small talk and keeping an ear out for the sound of Alex's key in the lock. After a while, Freddy began to squirm and misbehave. Danielle turned to Lynn and asked the nanny to put him to bed.

"Lynn will read you your story tonight, darling. Mommy's really tired. I love you, and I'll see you in the morning." She kissed her little boy and went to the sofa to put her feet up.

Don walked into the kitchen to tackle the dishes. Danielle thought to herself that this was a bizarre scene. Alex should be the one at home with her, putting Freddy to bed and doing the dishes. How could the medical students and their problems be more important than this?

In the kitchen, Don dialed Alex's cell phone, and when there was no answer, he left an urgent message and had him paged. There was still no response. Doctors don't ignore pages. He was alarmed. There was no logical reason for Alex to ignore his pages.

"Don," Danielle suddenly shouted from the living room. "My water broke. The baby's coming. Oh God! Please come in here and help me."

Don dropped the dish towel and ran into the living room. He gazed down at Danielle. He could see she was already in heavy labor, writhing in pain. "I'll ask Lynn to stay the night with Freddy, and then I'll drive you to the hospital. Hang on, Danielle. Don't worry. I'll be with you the whole time."

"Hurry please," she begged. "This baby is determined to make her appearance tonight. Where is Alex?" she moaned. "He needs to meet us in the delivery room."

"Of course. I'll call him," Don reassured her. It was so unlike Alex to be out of contact for so long, especially with a pregnant wife due to deliver at any minute. Something was terribly wrong. He didn't want to alarm Danielle, so he helped her into his car and broke all the speed limits getting her to the hospital.

CHAPTER 33

Darcy

Darcy was still reeling from the discovery of the lump in her right breast. Her heart raced, and she broke into a cold sweat whenever she allowed her mind to dwell on it and what it could mean for her health … her life. She wanted answers and right away.

Her gyn gave her a thorough physical examination and verified that he did feel a small lump in the lower outer quadrant of her right breast. Then he tried to reassure her that most growths in breast tissue were benign. But to be certain the lump wasn't cancerous, he ordered a 3-D mammogram and a breast ultrasound as the next diagnostic step. Once those results were read by a radiologist, he would discuss with Darcy and Mark what needed to be done next. The solution could be as easy as doing nothing or simply watching the lump and having another mammogram in a month to see whether it had grown. However, if her test results were suspicious, she may have to have an MRI and possibly a biopsy.

None of this news sounded good to Darcy, and she went through those first few days after finding the lump in a "controlled" state of panic. Luckily, she had her work to distract her except in the wee hours of the morning, when she could think of nothing else but getting the offending mass out of her body.

Scheduling the medical appointments in between her White House duties was tricky. She didn't want Connie or anyone at the White House to know what was going on. She planned to wait until she knew all the facts, and then she would decide who and how much to tell. Keeping such an important secret from Danielle killed her, but she didn't want to worry her sister unnecessarily. There was nothing anyone could do until she had a firm diagnosis. Then there would be enough time for hand-wringing or celebration.

Darcy was able to get the ultrasound and the mammography preformed at Georgetown Hospital the following day. But while she waited for the radiologist to read her films, she was tense and worried. In the meantime, even though she tried to be positive and put on a stoic face to the world, the fear of having breast cancer and its potential consequences were never far from her thoughts ... or Mark's.

She could never remember being so busy, not even when she'd been a realtor, who was constantly juggling clients, arranging showings, and attending closings; and not when she'd been a sportscaster writing scripts, interviewing athletes, and traveling around the country to film and promote *Speaking of Sports with Donavan & Donavan*.

* * *

After the inaugural festivities were concluded, the Pierce administration jumped full speed into its ambitious agenda. There were dozens of daily meetings in the East and West Wings or elsewhere and to-do lists that exceeded Darcy's phone gigabyte capacity. She now carried three different phones to handle all the various situations. She barely had time to think about her lump, but sometimes she found herself feeling her breast, hoping the lump had mysteriously disappeared. Of course, it hadn't.

She was constantly on the move, organizing, coordinating, and putting out fires. Her diplomatic skills were frequently tested when White House staff members pitted themselves against each other over sensitive issues. Darcy had to be the referee. Connie was in charge of hiring her own staff, but all the details of their employment, job descriptions, and accountability were left to Darcy.

The first week was so arduous that Darcy rarely went home. Much to Mark's displeasure, she spent several nights on a sofa in her office because her phones rang constantly, and she didn't want to keep her husband awake. Little did she realize that her breast mass was what was keeping her husband awake at night, not her ringing phone.

He was overwhelmed with work himself. The press corps and reporters weren't content with the three-times-a-week briefing from him. They demanded to know every detail of the president's activities and schedule. The administration was in its "honeymoon" period, but that didn't keep enthusiastic journalists from writing or broadcasting ridiculous stories.

One Pulitzer Prize-winning reporter took the time to write a scathing editorial in the *New York Times* about the president's unhealthy eating habits when he discovered Nathan had a cheeseburger every day for lunch. The meat activists were thrilled, but the vegetarian advocacy groups protested vehemently. Mark had to appease the ridiculous criticism by making the president's cholesterol scores, which were in the normal range, public. Darcy also had to counter the criticism by doing an interview, revealing Connie's favorite salad and meatless soup recipes on *Good Morning America* and *The Today Show*. The First Lady issued a statement that she enjoyed eating her greens and vegetables every day and rarely ate beef. The whole issue seemed silly and preposterous to Darcy and Mark, but handling things like that was part of their jobs. They had hoped to be more involved in important matters, but keeping disgruntled voters happy took up a lot of their time.

Darcy's doctor called with news. Her mammogram showed an irregularity inside one of her milk ducts. He told her he suspected she had DCIS (ductal carcinoma in situ), which was the earliest and most treatable form of breast cancer. It wasn't invasive, meaning that it hadn't spread, and was at a low risk of doing so. If this DCIS diagnosis was confirmed by a breast biopsy, Darcy would need to see a breast surgeon to determine the course of treatment and discuss all the options. Some breast cancers required no surgery, and other protocols suggested a lumpectomy followed by radiation and hormone therapy.

Darcy barely heard the rest of the conversation. She stood frozen in place and dropped the phone on the floor. Her worst nightmare was coming true. She pushed the intercom on her desk and asked her secretary to find Mark and send him to the office as soon as possible. In the meantime, she hugged herself and rocked slowly back and forth in a daze. She didn't cry. Her eyes burned, but no tears came. The lump in her throat was so big she could hardly swallow.

Mark took one look at her and knew she'd received bad news. He took her in his arms and rocked back and forth with her until she began to calm down. Then he led her to the sofa, and she told him everything the doctor had said.

***

They had to postpone the MRI because at the last minute the Pierces decided to attend a worldwide economic summit in Switzerland. Darcy and her staff were indispensable in coordinating and making most of the arrangements with Nathan's chief of staff, Warren Betts. The conference was expected to last three days and would involve many heads of state. Darcy's gyn pulled some strings and was able to reschedule her MRI for the day after she returned from the trip. The Pierce presential party left Washington on Air Force One for Zurich. Darcy and Mark were on board. No one knew Darcy's precarious state of health.

The meeting was contentious at first when the participants tried to deal with the mounting concerns about the global economic slowdown. Expectations for the meeting had been low, but surprisingly in the end, many issues had been resolved, and most analysts deemed the gathering to be a success. Nathan played a prominent role in the negotiations. The Pierces returned to Washington amid accolades from Wall Street pundits and praise from many economists. At Nathan's initiative, a trade deal with Japan had been made behind closed doors, and Mark proudly announced it as soon as Air Force One landed on American soil. It was February 14, Valentine's Day, but Darcy and Mark were too jet lagged to even notice.

"Where has all the time gone?" Darcy asked wearily on their way home. "It seems like only yesterday that Nathan called and offered us our jobs."

"I know, honey. But while this White House stuff has been a terrific experience, we've let things in our personal lives slide badly. After your MRI tomorrow, we're going to put your health first, no matter what. Nathan and Connie will understand, and they will have to function without us for a while if you need surgery or treatment. If they can't do that, then we'll have to resign. Our jobs are not that important. Your health trumps everything else." He took her hand and squeezed it affectionately. "Donavan and Donavan will get through this medical problem together just like we do everything else."

"I know," she said and squeezed his hand back. "And I feel so guilty. I've been so caught up in worry about this damn lump that I've neglected everything else, especially Danielle and her family. I can't believe it, but I haven't talked or texted her in almost two weeks, and her baby is due any day. Let's Facetime with her tomorrow, no matter what … even if we have a nuclear war." She joked. "And oh my God, I just realized that we never followed through on our dinner with the Three Stooges. Ginger must wonder why I've never called her after she told me about Jason's baby. I feel terrible."

Darcy was ashamed of herself. She wasn't normally self-centered, but this lump had changed everything. "I love my job, Mark, but it can't replace our family and friends."

"I have an idea," Mark offered. "Call Ginger and arrange a dinner for a few weeks from now, and in the morning, right after your procedure, we'll fly to New York and surprise Danielle and Alex with a quick visit. It will be much better than Facetiming them. God knows we both deserve a break and thinking about something other than your breast. I'm sure Nathan and Connie will give us a few days off."

CHAPTER 34

Danielle

Danielle barely made it to the hospital in time. Don pulled his car up to the emergency room entrance. Danielle was immediately taken to a labor suite. There was no time for the nurses to administer any anesthesia. Caroline Coulter Stone was in a hurry to be born and pushed her way into the world at nine thirty in the evening on Thursday, February 14, a Valentine's Day gift. Don March was at Danielle's bedside. Alex was not.

Danielle held the baby and cooed lovingly to her newborn daughter. The infant was adorable, everything any mother could have hoped for. But Danielle was miserable. "I don't understand this," she cried to Don. "Where in the world is Alex? I can't believe he's not answering his pages. You did try to call him, didn't you?"

Don squeezed her hand. He didn't answer her question because he had tried numerous times to reach Alex, with no luck. He was as angry and frustrated with his friend as Danielle was. His absence was inexcusable, and Don hated to see Danielle so justifiably upset. After Alex's callous indifference to his pregnant wife, Don thought he may have to rethink his loyalty to his friend and tell Danielle how he really felt about her.

"Now that I know you and the baby are okay, I'll get to the bottom of this. His pager battery probably died. There's got to be a reasonable explanation. Try to rest. I'll bring Alex to you as soon as I can track him down." He bent down and kissed her on the forehead, and he kissed the sleeping infant too.

Don left the maternity ward and marched angrily to Alex's office. He was seething. Alex didn't deserve a fine woman like Danielle. He had betrayed her in the worst way. Alex's office was empty, but his papers were scattered all over his desk, and there were several empty Starbucks coffee cups lined up on it. Don noticed a "World's Best Doctor" mug on a nearby shelf along with several pictures of Danielle and Freddy and a few of Darcy and Mark. He tried calling Alex's cell and his pager, again with the same negative result.

Something was terribly wrong. Don knew it in his bones. If Alex didn't show up by morning, he was going to call the police and report him missing. His unexplained absence was torture for Danielle—and so cruel. Don was furious with his friend for putting Danielle through this agony and for missing the birth of his precious child. *I'd give my right arm to have Rachelle and Carly back*, he thought morosely. *How can Alex willingly neglect his wonderful wife and baby?*

Don went back to the maternity ward to check on Danielle. She was asleep with the baby lying in the bassinette next to her. He slipped quietly into the room and fell into a fitful sleep in the chair next to her bedside. It was as if he were standing guard over them in anticipation of something horrendous about to happen.

Several hours later, he was awakened by a police officer standing in the doorway, accompanied by Danielle's physician. "Sorry to wake you," the doctor said in a choked voice. "Danielle, I'm so sorry, but I have terrible news."

Don jumped out of his chair and went to Danielle's bedside. She looked up at him, fear in her eyes. He gently took her hand. "What's wrong?" she asked the policeman in a shaking voice. "Is it Alex?"

"Yes, I'm afraid so," the doctor said sadly. "Your husband's body was discovered by hospital security an hour ago. He was sitting behind the wheel of his car in the hospital parking lot. The ignition was still running. There was a bouquet of pink flowers on the front seat, and the whole back of the car was filled with 'Congratulations, it's a girl' balloons. We won't know officially until there's an autopsy, but it appears that Dr. Stone suffered a massive heart attack and died instantly."

Danielle's started to shake, and her eyes filled with tears. She could barely breathe. She looked desperately back and forth between the doctor and Don. This had to be a nightmare. "That can't be true. Alex is fine. There has to be a mistake. We just had a baby, for God's sake."

Don held her as she shook violently and rocked back and forth in agony. "Please tell me it's a mistake," she begged. "I need to see Alex. I want to see my husband now!"

She glanced over at the bassinette. At the sight of her sleeping newborn daughter, she broke into heartbreaking, uncontrollable sobs.

CHAPTER 35

Darcy

Darcy and Mark left the hospital after her MRI and flew to LaGuardia Airport. They arrived at 11:00 a.m. and took an Uber directly to their condo. They'd brought no luggage, since everything they needed was already in their apartment there. They were burdened down instead with multiple gifts for Freddy, Valentine's candy for the whole Stone family, and an assortment of baby gifts Darcy had been collecting since moving to DC. The latest acquisition was an authentic swiss cuckoo clock she'd bought in Zurich during one of her few free moments on her recent trip. She knew Freddy would love it.

"I am so excited to see everyone," Darcy said to Mark as she impatiently rang Danielle's doorbell. "Danielle will be so surprised, and I can't wait to see little Freddy."

A woman Darcy didn't recognize opened the apartment door. "Oh my, it's like seeing a ghost," the woman blurted out. "You have to be Ms. Danielle's twin."

"Yes, I am," Darcy answered. "And you are?"

"Oh, sorry. I'm Lynn, the Stones' nanny. Come in." She moved aside so Darcy and Mark could enter the apartment. Darcy noticed Hippocrates standing guard under the stairwell and laughed. It looked like Freddy had tried to put a diaper on him but hadn't been able to get it over his legs.

"Aunt Darcy, Unk Mark." Freddy squealed with delight when he saw them and jumped into their arms. "I didn't know you were coming."

"We wanted to make it a surprise." Mark smiled at the adorable little boy. "Are you happy to see us? And where's your mommy?"

"She's with the baby," Lynn said, her voice cracking with emotion.

"The baby?" Darcy gasped. "My sister had the baby? Caroline is here already?"

"Yes, ma'am. The determined little rascal arrived last night. The doctors wanted to keep Ms. Danielle in the hospital for a few days because of the shock, but she insisted on coming home early this morning to be with Master Freddy. Dr. March brought her home, and they're both in the nursery now. Ms. Danielle's been trying to nurse, but she's so upset and emotional that her milk hasn't come in, and the poor little baby's practically starving. They've just asked me to go to the drug store and pick up some formula. It's all so sad. I still can't believe what's happened."

"Wait a minute." Darcy was confused. "I don't understand any of this. Why is Danielle in shock and upset? Why did Don bring her home and not Alex?"

Freddy tugged at the packages in Darcy's arms. "Aunt Darcy, are those for me?" he asked innocently.

"Yes, darling. They're mostly for you, but some are for your little sister." She handed the packages to the nanny. "Freddy, where's your daddy?"

Lynn tried to answer, to soften the blow, since it was obvious Darcy knew nothing about the recent tragedy. However, Freddy, being only a three-year-old, blurted out exactly what he'd been told only hours ago. "Mommy says Daddy went to heaven last night, and now he's our special angel with God, and he's looking out for Mommy, the baby, and me."

CHAPTER 36

Danielle

Danielle held the infant to her breast as uncontrolled tears streamed down her face. "I hear your voices out there, Darcy, but I just can't make myself get up." Her words were barely coherent as she sobbed. "I can't believe Alex is gone. He never got to see the baby." Danielle's whole body shook with unimaginable grief. She was inconsolable.

Darcy went running to her twin sister's side and knelt down beside her. "Oh my God, Danielle. I don't know what to say. This is terrible."

Don March stood up and backed away from the two heartbroken women. "You two need to be alone now." He reached down and gently took the baby from Danielle's arms. "I'll be right outside with Caroline." He quietly left the room, cradling the infant.

Returning to the living room, he said hello to Mark, and the two men sat down to talk. Don explained as much as he could about what had happened and said that they thought Alex had had a massive and fatal heart attack the night before and was pronounced dead in the emergency room at about the same time Danielle was giving birth. The whole story was so heart-wrenchingly sad that Don could hardly get the words out. He told Mark that Alex had become his closest friend since he had begun working with Danielle at Healing Words. He also told Mark that he cared deeply for Danielle and would do everything in his power to be of help to her, Freddy, and the baby in the days, weeks, and months ahead.

He had endured his own overwhelming grief, so he knew what Danielle would have to face in the future.

Mark was stunned. He adored Danielle and respected Alex deeply. They had spent almost every day and evening together for the last five years until he and Darcy moved to DC. "The world will be a sadder place without Alex Stone in it," he said with profound grief. "Is it too soon to ask if any funeral arrangements have been made?"

"No. Not yet," Don answered quietly. "Danielle is so weak and in so much anguish, I don't think she can handle making the plans. Would you be willing to help me work out the details?"

"Yes, of course," Mark answered solemnly. "Normally Darcy would step right in and take over. Organization is her thing. She and Alex were exceptionally close too. This will be very hard on her."

"Excuse me, Dr. March," Lynn interrupted timidly. "I need to go to the store to get the baby's formula. Should I take Freddy or leave him here with you?"

"Why don't you take him and maybe swing by the park for just a little bit of fresh air? The less of this sorrow and crying he's sees, the better," Don answered but looked to Mark for approval.

"I agree, and Freddy," Mark said, turning to the boy, "your nanny's going to take you out for a bit. Aunt Darcy and I will be here when you get back, and we'll open the presents we brought you and the baby."

Freddy was so happy that he had a baby sister and that Aunt Darcy and Unk Mark were there. He didn't understand why everyone was so sad and crying. He was happy to go on an outing with Nanny Lynn. "Bye-bye." He waved. "Be back for presents soon."

Mark and Don began to make lists and phone calls, planning the viewing and the funeral service. Mark excused himself to call Nathan and Connie. They would want to attend the service, and he had to ask for more time off for Darcy and himself. He went back to Don and explained that the president and the First Lady would be attending the service. That detail threw another wrinkle into the mix. The secret service would have some specific demands and requirements.

"I guess we should try to keep Danielle and Darcy out of this planning as much as possible. That will make it easier on them," Mark said soberly.

"This is so bloody awful." He pulled out his handkerchief and dabbed at his eyes. "I'll miss Alex very much. He was the best man in our wedding and was truly my best friend."

"And we have to make sure Danielle rests as much as possible. She gave birth less than twenty-four hours ago. I don't want her to hemorrhage or have complications." Don was very concerned. "She's a strong woman, but a tragedy like this can break the best of us."

The men continued to talk and make arrangements for the funeral to be held in three days. An hour later Lynn brought Freddy home and put him down for a nap. She handed the formula to Dr. March, and he began to feed the baby with the formula bottle's nipple. Darcy and Danielle stayed in the nursery, clutching each other, crying, praying, and trying to grasp what had happened.

Finally, Don and Mark went into the nursery and brought the two twins into the living room. Lynn had made them sandwiches, which they barely touched. Danielle was so exhausted that she could barely move. Don eventually helped her into her bedroom, the room she'd shared with Alex … and that started another round of heartbreaking sobs. Darcy held her sister tightly, and the two crawled onto the bed together, holding onto each other tightly. Their twin bond was both emotional and physical.

"I want to sleep now and never wake up," Danielle sobbed. "I can't do this, Darcy. I can't live without Alex."

CHAPTER 37

Danielle and Darcy

Danielle and Darcy clutched each other's hand in mutual anguish. Shaking with unimaginable sorrow, they stood silently side by side and watched in disbelief as the shiny mahogany casket was lowered into the ground. Neither could force her eye to look anywhere else. They fought gallantly to control their emotions and to support each other in their grief. Their sadness was so profound, emotions so raw, that they couldn't even begin to acknowledge the well-meaning condolences from the dozens of prominent mourners who had traveled from all around the country to attend the burial service.

President Nathan Pierce stood solemnly at Danielle's right, and Mark supported Darcy at her left. Freddy, dressed in a little navy-blue sports jacket and striped tie beneath a chestnut wool overcoat, stood directly in front of his mother and aunt. He clutched a single white rose. In the row directly behind them, Connie, Don March, and Lynn struggled to keep their composure. The assembled group of mourners included doctors from all over the country who had studied with or been colleagues of Alex. His Boston and New York Hospital friends stood by helplessly as their fellow physician, friend, and mentor was lowered into the ground. The minister made the appropriate short speech about Alex being with God and in a better place, but hardly anyone was paying attention to his words or to the Bible passages he read. They were all lost in their private recollections of the very special man being buried.

Finally, the service ended, and each of the first two rows of mourners individually approached the coffin, said a private prayer, and dropped a single rose on it. Darcy, Danielle, and Freddy went last. The scene was so poignant that sobs could be heard emitting from throughout the crowd. Darcy looked down at the coffin and remembered how instrumental Alex had been in reuniting her and Danielle. He had given her back her sister. She would always love him and be grateful. She made a silent promise that she and Mark would always look after his family— Danielle, Freddy, and Caroline.

Danielle went next. Her heart was so heavy, and she was in excruciating emotional pain. She stared blankly at the coffin, unable to believe the man she loved and the father of her two children lay cold and dead inside. The thought was too much. The heart-wrenching sobs exploded from her body, her knees buckled, and she collapsed to the cold ground in grief. Don ran over to her and held her until the sobbing stopped. When she was calmer, he led her slowly back to Darcy's side, where the two twins hugged each other as if they would never let go.

Freddy seemed to know it was his turn. He looked at Unk Mark for approval and then walked slowly to the hole in the ground. Looking down, he dropped his single white rose onto his father's coffin. "I love you, Dada," he said, unaware of the enormity of the moment. "Don't worry. Hipps and I will take care of Mommy and baby Caroline."

The minister gave the benediction, and one by one the mourners left the gravesite to return to their lives. Only the president and Mrs. Pierce, with their secret service protection, and Darcy, Mark, Danielle, Don, and Freddy lingered behind.

"I can't leave him here all alone, so cold and locked in that horrid box," Danielle wailed. "I just can't!"

"I understand, honey." Connie put her arm around her good friend, trying to comfort her. "But Alex would want you to be strong ... to take care of yourself so you can watch over Freddy and Caroline for him. You have to believe that Alex is no longer here on earth but in a better, peaceful place."

"That's right," Don concurred. "And you need to be at home, taking care of that precious baby. That's what Alex would want. He always believed in you, in your amazing strength. He was so proud of you. Now you must show him that he was right. You have to carry on as he would want you to." He gently pulled her toward the line of limousines parked behind them, waiting to take the mourners home.

"Wait." Danielle broke away and walked determinedly back to the gravesite with her head held high. "Alex, my darling," she said forlornly to the coffin in the ground, "I don't know how I can go on without you, but I promise I'll do my best to be a good mother to our children and keep your memory alive for them. In the future, I need you to send me a sign, a signal of some sort, to let me know that you think I'm doing the right things and that you're proud of me. I need you to do that for me, please, my love, please."

She looked for the last time at his mahogany coffin. "I love you beyond words. Rest in peace, my darling Alex. Rest in peace."

Part 3

CHAPTER 38

Darcy and Danielle

Danielle barely survived the next few weeks after Alex's death. She struggled to get through the days, but the nights were pure torture.

In the daylight hours, she tried to keep herself busy with the children, particularly the baby. Caroline ate every three hours and was colicky. Freddy was cranky, and he missed his father enormously. He was also jealous of the attention Caroline received. The three-year-old boy couldn't understand why his father wasn't home. With no religious training, he didn't understand the concept of heaven and kept going over to Hippocrates and asking the family statue, "Where's Dada?" He was lonely and confused and often curled up in a ball, crying, and slept at the statue's feet.

At night Danielle wandered around the apartment, unable to sleep, and when she finally dozed off, she tossed and turned and had terrible nightmares, in which she lost Alex again and again. She woke sobbing and utterly exhausted. She tried to hide her grief and tears during the day so Freddy wouldn't see her crying, but when she was alone, the pain, the loss, and her despair poured out. She was devastated and very angry at God for taking Alex from her so soon.

Darcy had requested a six-week leave of absence from her White House job to stay in New York to help Danielle. Connie had readily agreed. Mark returned to DC a few days after the funeral but flew up to be with Darcy and Danielle every weekend. It wasn't the way they had thought their White House jobs would begin. Nothing had gone according to plan. For once, Darcy didn't feel in control, and this scared her. She couldn't make everything all right for her sister, and she wouldn't do anything about her own health issues until she felt it was all right to leave Danielle and return home.

Darcy did whatever she could to make the day-to-day chores following Alex's death easier for Danielle. She took on the task of assembling all Alex's financial papers and delivering his will to Alex's attorney. She had been named as one of the executors of his estate. Alex's will was simple and straightforward. He left everything to Danielle, including the condo, all his assets, and his personal belongings. With Darcy's competence, she quickly completed all the necessary paperwork so all Danielle had to do was sign a few documents.

The next task was to go through Alex's things, his clothes and his personal items. She donated his clothing to a veterans' association and dispensed the other items to charities or discarded them. Danielle left this onerous task completely up to Darcy. She swore she couldn't touch Alex's things. It was too painful. "I want to remember him," she had pleaded with her sister, "but I can't stand to see his hairbrush or his razor. They make me so sad."

Darcy understood completely. She knew people reacted differently in times of grief. Some kept the deceased closet filled and their personal items around for years, as a kind of shrine. Others, like Danielle, wanted to get rid of everything physical and keep only their memories. Photos were the exception. Danielle put pictures of Alex everywhere ... on every available surface. She wanted Freddy to always remember what his father had looked like. When Caroline was older, she would get to know him through Danielle's stories and his photographs too.

Danielle hadn't left the apartment since the funeral. It had been over three weeks. She had no desire to go anywhere or see anyone. She didn't care about having her hair or nails done or even about what she wore. Many days she stayed in her pajamas and bedroom slippers, and showered only when Darcy lovingly nagged her. She had no reason to look pretty, no one to dress up for, and there was no one she wanted to be with except Darcy. Danielle was clothed in misery and grief, in darkness and despair. Even Don couldn't get through to her, although he was by her side every day, helping any way he could.

Everything reminded Danielle of her terrible loss. She couldn't be distracted from thoughts of Alex. Don tried to get her to come to the Healing Words offices, but she refused. She had lost interest in its work. Darcy urged her to take Freddy for a walk, but she wouldn't make the effort. Instead she sat huddled in the corner of the sofa, the side where Alex always sat, and looked endlessly at pictures of him. In her mind she relived every moment of their marriage, the happy times and the not-so-good ones. She was afraid that if she forgot a single detail of her life with Alex, she would lose even more of her beloved husband. She was frozen in time and had no desire to move on.

Freddy begged his mommy to read to him, watch a movie, or play a game. She always made excuses and sent him to be with Lynn or Darcy. Freddy was confused and very lonely. He had lost his daddy, and now his mommy was slipping away. It was frightening for a little boy. He cried himself to sleep at night and missed the family he had always known.

Darcy finally realized she and Don couldn't pull Danielle out of her profound depression. She called Danielle's former therapist and friend, Dr. Ray Smith, and asked for his help. She explained how Danielle was acting and begged him to come to New York to see her. He readily agreed. He hadn't seen Danielle since Alex's funeral, and he wanted to help her. He tried to reach her many times by phone, but she never took his calls. Using the Healing Words business as an excuse, he flew to New York and arrived on Danielle's front door unannounced.

CHAPTER 39

Danielle

Danielle was alone in the apartment with the baby. Darcy had gone to Alex's office that morning to clear out his things and bring home whatever she thought Danielle might want. Lynn was grocery shopping with Freddy.

The doorbell rang. Danielle was startled. She wasn't expecting anyone and didn't feel up to visitors. This was her quiet time with Caroline, and she cherished it. She was continuously in awe of her beautiful daughter and counting her tiny toes and fingers for the hundredth time. She desperately wished Alex had lived to see his gorgeous little daughter. Life was so unfair, and Danielle was still so angry.

Dr. Smith walked into the apartment as soon as Danielle opened the door. He didn't wait for an invitation to enter or to hear her excuses about why she was too busy to see him. "We need to talk," he stated boldly. "And right now."

"Well, look what the cat dragged in," Danielle said, greeting her old friend. "I don't suppose this is a coincidence. You just happened to be in the neighborhood? Did Darcy or Don put you up to this?" She felt set up.

"The who isn't important, Danielle. It's the why."

"I know," she said meekly. "I've been a basket case, and I admit it. I guess I've alarmed everyone around me. It's just that I never thought I'd be raising two children by myself at thirty-six years old. I expected that Alex would be around to help until I was at lease ninety. And now

I can't face the next hour without him, much less the next day or week. Sometimes I wish I'd died instead of my husband."

"You don't really mean that." He looked stern. "And what about Freddy and Caroline? You know you love them, and they need you to be their mother."

"Darcy would raise them. She'll make a great mother," Danielle answered defensively. "Better than me under the present circumstances."

"Don't you think that's pretty selfish?" He looked at her intently. "Danielle, what you've been through is worse than horrible, but you, my dear friend, don't have the luxury of basking in your sorrow. You are not on an isolated island. People depend on you. Real life demands your attention. You *cannot* keep hiding from your pain. You must learn to deal with it.

"Of course, you'll grieve Alex now and perhaps forever, but you can't stop living. Your children need you. Your friends and colleagues count on you. Your wonderful program, Healing Words, needs your stewardship. Darcy would be devasted without you, and most importantly, you owe yourself the chance to glorify your wonderful husband's unselfish work and preserve his legacy. He made a wonderful commitment and convinced the senior staff of the hospital to take on individual medical students and mentor them throughout their entire medical school training and into the future. That was quite an undertaking. Alex gave his heart and soul to that effort. Do not let his dream die with him. It would make what happened to him a double tragedy."

"Oh my God." She started to sob. "You are so right. I want to be the best mother I can for my children, and I do have to honor Alex by ensuring that all his mentoring dreams continue and come true. Thank you, Ray. You are a wise man and a dear friend. I needed that kick in my butt. Once again you've shown me the way out of my darkest hours and given me some hope. I will try not to let you and Alex down, but I don't know where to begin." She looked at him forlornly. "I am lost."

"You don't have to do this alone," he emphasized. "You have support all around you. The hospital staff adored Alex, and they will help you in any way you want. From what I can see, Dr. March adores you also and was a good friend to Alex. Tap his energy and listen to his suggestions.

I believe he was the first doctor to sign up to be one of Alex's mentors. He'll know what you should do. And most importantly, throw yourself behind his program and make it yours as well. You will never regret it, and eventually this pain you feel will subside and turn into joy because you'll have finished the great work your husband began."

Daniele stood up and embraced the man who had filled her heart with so much wisdom. "Thank you, Ray." She smiled, really smiled, for the first time since Alex's death. "You've given me a lot to think about, and beginning right now, I'm going to be a new woman, one whom Alex would be proud to call his wife."

"He was always proud of you, Danielle," Dr. Smith replied emotionally. He saw that she had made a real breakthrough. "I know he told you that every day. Now you just have to remember it and act accordingly."

They hugged again. "Call me if you need me," Dr. Smith said as he left the apartment. "I'm always here for you, but I honestly think you're going to be all right now."

Danielle sat down in the silent apartment, reflecting on all Dr. Smith had said. She picked up Caroline, holding her close to her breasts, and whispered tenderly, "I love you, my precious little baby, and Mommy will always take care of you and make you and your daddy proud."

When Freddy and Lynn returned with the groceries and Darcy walked in, carrying two large cardboard boxes from Alex's office, Danielle looked up at them with love and a genuine smile. The troubled, anguished expression was gone. Love shone brightly in her eyes. "How about a pizza and a movie?"

Darcy looked at her sister tenderly. Tears of happiness glistened in her eyes. She didn't know what Dr. Smith had said, but whatever it was, it had done the trick and brought Danielle back to life. Freddy sensed a change too and ran to his mother to hug her. He could see she was feeling better because she was laughing and smiling like she used to before Dada went to heaven.

"I guess it's time for me to go back to Washington." Darcy smiled. "I think everything's going to be just fine here."

"Yes, I suppose in time it will be." Danielle nodded. "Some days will be better than others, but I'm going to try to keep a positive attitude. The kids deserve that. Thanks for everything you've done, Darcy. I couldn't have gotten through this terrible time without you. I'll always miss my husband and wish he were here with us, but thanks to you and Don and Ray Smith, the Stone family is not only going to survive, but we will flourish."

I hope the same can be said about me and my damn lump, Darcy thought anxiously. *It's time I go home, get the MRI results, and face the music.*

CHAPTER 40

Darcy

Darcy returned to DC in early April. The ground was still frozen, and the skies were bleak, exactly as she felt. Alex had been an important person in her life, and she would always miss him. At least she felt comforted that Danielle would be all right in time and had Dr. Smith and Don March as supportive and caring friends. She planned to return to New York as often as she and Mark could get away from their White House responsibilities, but now she had to concentrate on her health. Her doctor felt a breast biopsy was the next logical step. He didn't want to leave any loose ends.

So, on her first day back at work, Darcy and Mark went to the hospital during their lunch hour for her biopsy. She still hadn't told anyone about her lump and the suspected DCIS. She was nervous and scared, not by the uncomfortable procedure but by the possible results. She had been surrounded by the consequences of death for the last few weeks and couldn't allow herself to think about her own mortality.

Mark was by her side. He was as anxious as she was but tried not to show it. He went into a nearby room to wait, while a nurse helped Darcy change into a hospital gown.

Once inside the room where the biopsy would be performed, a male technician stood in front of her and began drawing on her right breast with a surgical magic marker to pinpoint the diameter and location of the lump. When he was finished, she was instructed to lie facedown on a huge metal table with holes cut out where she was supposed to position her breasts. It was a very uncomfortable and awkward position. Then the table was mechanically lifted higher so the surgeon could work from beneath it. There was nothing dignified or modest about the prep or the procedure. Darcy didn't care. She was beyond being embarrassed and only wanted to get the whole ordeal over with and hopefully avoid surgery.

Soon after she and the table were in position, the surgeon, Dr. Ira Mask, walked into the room, greeted Darcy warmly, and began to talk as he numbed an area of her right breast and went about the business of removing a chunk of her tissue where the technician had marked it. He continued to talk to her calmly and explained everything that he was doing step-by-step. The tissue would be preserved in formaldehyde and paraffin, and then frozen and cut into thins slices to be examined under the microscope. He said he had to remove enough tissue so it reached the edges (margins) of the lump. "If enough tissue is not extracted," he continued soberly, "the cancer can be overlooked, which happens about twenty percent of the time. Don't worry. I'll take enough tissue for an accurate diagnosis, but you won't be disfigured in any way."

Darcy hadn't thought about disfigurement. She wanted the lump and any cancerous cells around it removed once and for all. Her life versus her breast; it was a no brainer.

When the procedure was finished, she was left with a badly swollen and bruised breast and one tiny stich. Then the hard part began … waiting for the pathology report.

CHAPTER 41

Darcy and Connie

Darcy returned to the White House the next day for her usual 8:00 a.m. meeting with Connie. What she learned was disturbing. The First Lady quickly brought her up to speed about all that had happened in DC during Darcy's six-week absence. She explained that the administration was being barraged by negative press, both political and personal, and that a raunchy tabloid had printed a story implying that Nathan and Darcy were having an ongoing affair in the Oval Office.

"What?" Darcy was outraged. "Oh, Connie, I'm so sorry. You must believe me. It's not true! I adore you and Nathan. I would never cross that line, and neither would your husband."

"Of course. I know that." Connie's voice cracked, and her eyes glistened with unfallen tears. "But the stories are so hurtful to us all. Nathan is devasted, and I know Mark is furious. We have to find a way to squash those rumors."

She reached over and took Darcy's hand. "Mark didn't want to worry you with this while you were taking care of Danielle, but now that you are back in town, it's time to face the problem head-on."

"Anything, Connie. I will do anything to help." Darcy couldn't remember ever being so angry except when Mark had been unjustifiably fired from the network.

At his regular press briefings, Mark had done his best to deflect the rumors and concentrate on the administration's positive talking points on domestic and foreign policies. But insensitive and rude reporters continued to question him about the "supposed affair." Mark was furious and always on the defensive.

When in New York, Darcy had talked to her husband nightly, but she had no idea about these scurrilous rumors casting her as an adulteress and President Pierce as a philanderer. She was shocked and horrified.

She had read about the press's discord with the administration's policies in the *Times* and other newspapers, but she had no idea how serious the consequences were for the administration's plans or that she was specifically named in some of the scandalous rumors. Mark had lovingly kept that information from her, afraid she was too fragile after Alex's death and from the stress of worrying about her own health. But now that Connie had told her the whole truth, Darcy was devasted by the injustice and inflammatory nature of the rumors and innuendos. She was determined to put a stop to them and repair her reputation and Nathan's.

"I have an idea," Darcy said soberly. "Can we meet with Nathan and Mark later today, and I'll tell you all what I have in mind? I can't control how the press frames it's criticism of the administration's policies, but I damn well can control what they say about me. My plan's a little out of the box, but I think it might work."

Finally, when the meeting ended, Connie looked at Darcy and chuckled. "There's also some rather shocking news I heard from Nathan's sister. I'm pretty sure you may already know about it." She rolled her eyes in dismay. "Ginger informed us that, at the ripe old age of eighty, she's going to become a mother figure to Jason and Edward's child. I feel so sorry for the poor kid."

"I know," Darcy commiserated. "Mark and I think it's crazy too, but you can't shove toothpaste back into the tube once it's been squeezed out. It's too late for that. The baby's coming, so I guess having Ginger as a mother figure is better than having no mother at all."

"I suppose when you put it like that. I still can't believe Edward went along with the surrogacy thing." Connie shook her head in disbelief.

"Apparently it was his idea. Mark thinks Edward did it to honor Jason."

"That's probably true, but couldn't he have had a statue of Jason made instead?" Connie replied sarcastically. She was dumbfounded that her sister-in-law was so eager to take on this maternal responsibility, especially since she'd done such a lousy job of raising her own child."

Darcy looked at Connie. "Mark and I are going to have Edward for dinner one night soon and offer to help in some way. The poor man has no idea what's ahead, and partnering with Ginger will be no walk in the park for him."

"You got that right." Connie snickered. "Now let's forget about the nasty rumors, the damn press, and Ginger's folly for a minute and tell me … how is Danielle doing, really? I'm so worried about her."

CHAPTER 42

Danielle

Danielle forced herself to go back to the Healing Words offices at the end of May, a little more than three months since Alex had passed. She struggled with leaving her children at home with Lynn, because since losing her husband so unexpectedly, she was irrationally afraid that something awful might happen to her children too. She knew she was being overprotective but couldn't help it. She wouldn't survive another loss.

For the last month, she had taken Dr. Smith's words to heart and talked with Don over and over again about how to advance Alex's mentoring program and how to best honor his memory.

Dr. Smith had kept in frequent touch with Danielle and visited her often. Knowing she needed professional help, he referred her to a Manhattan psychiatrist, Dr. Dorian. She had been seeing him three times a week. He was helping her to cope with what had happened to Alex and to move her life forward without him. Day by day, she was becoming a little stronger, crying a little less, and gradually returning to her old self. She had been forced by terrible circumstances to accept her new role as a single parent, with all the responsibilities it entailed. She still missed Alex all the time, but the crushing sense of loss was slowly fading, and with Dr. Dorian's help, it was being replaced by doing things that would have made Alex proud.

Don was by her side almost constantly, both at home and at the office. His feelings for Danielle were intense, and he had fallen deeply in love with her. However, he still kept his affection for her to himself, because she was still grieving and not ready for any new emotional commitments. He was proud of the way she was surviving and mothering her two children, and he offered to be around as much or as little as she wanted.

"Healing Words is running beautifully," he said to her one morning. "The staff can manage the day-to-day decisions by themselves now, and I am continuing to look for more potential locations for additional chapters. As you recall, when I first joined you, we had fourteen. Now we have twenty-eight with number twenty-nine and thirty almost ready to go."

"I know. It's amazing," Danielle reflected proudly. "From one spiral notebook to this amazing writing program. It's hard to wrap my mind around how successful it's become and how many patients we've helped."

"You should be proud, Danielle. They number in the thousands now. I think I've come up with a way we can reach even more people and just tweak the program a little to honor Alex."

"What do you mean?" She poured herself a cup of coffee and sat opposite him in his office (her old one). She loved how they bounced ideas off each other. He was so easy to talk to. "What needs tweaking?" She crossed her long legs, and his eyes took in the sensual sight. She didn't realize how provocative she was and that she exuded sensuality.

"I was thinking that you and I have talked so often about how to honor Alex and continue his mentoring program." He forced his eyes to look away from her long legs and focus on the stack of papers on his desk.

"Yes?" She was curious.

"What would you think of incorporating the general concept of writing down your feelings like our patients do now ... but also expanding the outreach of the program to include the medical students? Actually, the idea could apply to all students everywhere. They pretty much have the same worries about grades, passing tests, fear of failure, not getting into the right colleges or medical specialty, etcetera. We could develop a sister program for mentors and mentees. In addition to the personal, one-on-one meetings between a medical student, intern, or resident with a senior staff member, the young professionals would write down their concerns and share them with their peers in a group meeting, supervised by a Healing Words staff member."

"Wow." Danielle was impressed. "What a great idea. But do you think the medical students would go along with it?"

"Yes, I think so, because if they were willing to be a part of Alex's mentoring program, then this would just be another extension the program offers them ... and, as we know, it's a mighty powerful tool to help them cope with their stresses."

Danielle's mind spun with the possibilities. "We already have the Healing Words programs in so many hospitals. We can add this new mentoring one in the same locations and not have to worry about finding additional space to rent."

"Exactly. And think about what a benefit this would be for the staff doctors who volunteer to be the mentors. They have been uncertain of what they should do and say. Alex did a superb job of guiding them while he was alive, but now in his absence you could take over and guide the program yourself ... Maybe make up new lesson guides with videos dealing with their special medical student issues. As a doctor, you know exactly what they're going through, because you've been there. Having your videos at their fingertips will make it so much easier for the mentors to be effective."

Danielle was exuberant about Don's idea. "Let me think about this," she said. "But Don, thank you. I believe Alex would agree and be proud of us for carrying on his dream." She wanted to do everything in her power to keep her husband and his contributions from being forgotten. She had been married to a remarkable man.

Danielle looked at her watch and realized it was time for her to get home to her children. They were her main priority these days.

"Do you want me to drive you home?" Don asked. He would do anything to spend more time with Danielle, and he loved being around Caroline and Freddy.

"No, thanks. I'd like to walk. It'll give me time to think about this new concept before I'm back in diaper mode again." She waved at him, grabbed her purse, and headed outside.

That evening she fed and bathed the children and read Freddy his bedtime story. Then she poured herself a glass of Malbec, sat on the sofa while looking at Hippocrates for inspiration, and dialed Don's number.

"I've been thinking," she began without any preamble. "Doctors pride themselves on their ability to heal, and surgeons like Alex depend on their skilled hands. What if we call Alex's mentoring program 'Healing Hands,' the sister program of Healing Words ... the 'words' curriculum for patients with serious illnesses and the 'hands' curriculum for medical trainees and mentoring doctors?"

"I think it's a winner. An absolute winner, Danielle." *And so are you,* he thought longingly. *So are you, my darling.*

CHAPTER 43

Darcy

Darcy and Mark walked bravely into her breast surgeon's office. They were prepared for bad news but tried to remain stoic. Dr. Mask smiled at them as he shared the fantastic news that Darcy did *not* have cancer. Her breast lump was benign, not malignant. Her pathology report was clean, and she had every reason to believe that she'd lead a long and breast-cancer-free life. No one but God could 100 percent make that promise, but as long as Darcy kept up with frequent mammograms and did her monthly self-examinations, he assured her, she should be fine.

Both Mark and Darcy teared up with relief at the good news. They had been through a frightening time of worry and uncertainty but now saw hope and joy in their future. They thanked the doctor profoundly and left his office, gleefully holding hands.

When they got home, they opened a bottle of French champagne and agreed to take a few days off from work to celebrate. They also decided to keep Darcy's breast cancer scare private. Danielle and their friends all had enough to worry about. The news was good anyway, so what would be the point? They said a prayer, thanking God for Darcy's good health, and Mark gently caressed her breast. "Nice to have you back," he joked. "I've missed you."

Darcy spent the next morning at the spa, having her hair and nails done and enjoying a full-body massage. Now she was finishing setting the dining room table. Mark was opening the wine to let it breathe. They were expecting Edward for dinner. Ginger and Lloyd had declined their invitation, because they had a charity function to attend. Ginger was bound and determined to attend every social event she could before she became, in her own words, a "stay-at-home mom."

Edward, a sophisticated, Renaissance man—cultured, well read; and an avid art collector—had been devoted to Jason. Darcy and Mark adored him and had helped him recover emotionally after Jason died in a fiery plane crash seven years ago. Darcy had been the one to tell Ginger that her only son, Jason, was gay and had taken a lover and eventually married him. Jason had never had the nerve to tell his parents the truth about his sexuality. At first Ginger had been in denial, but with Darcy's gentle prodding, she came to accept Edward as a part of her son's life. He had been so kind and loving to Jason. How could she not be grateful to him?

The three of them were enjoying a leisurely dinner and chatting about Darcy and Mark's White House jobs. Darcy couldn't hold back any longer. She turned to Edward. "How are you going to manage a baby on your own at your age?" she asked bluntly.

"I was wondering how long it would take you to bring up the baby?" He smiled knowingly. "Let me assure you that before I agreed to find a surrogate to carry Jason's baby, I gave it a lot of thought and did a huge amount of research."

"I'm sure you did," Mark interjected. "But no amount of research will change the fact that you're seventy years old, which means you will be eighty-five when the baby is ready to get his driver's license. How do you think you'll have the energy at that age to raise a teenager?"

"God will provide. He always does," Edward answered soberly. He wasn't concerned in the least. "Fortunately, I have enough money to hire full-time help around the clock, if necessary. Lots of grandparents end up raising their grandkids for one reason or another. I don't see why I can't do it too. Besides, Ginger and Lloyd are going to help out when they can."

"I'm sure they will," Darcy answered in frustration. "But they're ten years older than you! How much help can they really be?"

"They can love the baby! That's the most important thing. And don't be so quick to dismiss us senior citizens. We have a lot of knowledge and experience to pass on to the next generation. I don't have to worry about making a living, so I won't be tied up in the office until all hours of the day and night or taking extended business trips. I will be home with my child all the time. That's more than either of you can say about your own parents."

"You've got me there," Darcy reluctantly agreed. "But it's still going to be difficult." She looked at Edward cautiously. She didn't want to overstep or jeopardize their friendship. "Mark and I have talked, and we're willing to pitch in when we can. Maybe take the baby to soccer or football practices or if it's a girl to ballet or music lessons … even to Disney for a few days, if you'll allow it. It would be our pleasure to help out."

"Of course, I will allow it. It would be great for the kid to be around you two, but don't you think you're being a little sexist? Girls play soccer nowadays, and boys like ballet and music. I think you've fallen for a stereotype."

"Yes, you're absolutely right," Mark interrupted, laughing. "But you know what we mean. Forgive us. Our intentions are good."

"Yes, I do. And thank you very much. I will accept all the help I can get. And Darcy, I know Jason would be thrilled to know you'll be involved in raising his baby. After all, if circumstances were different, this baby might have been yours. Kind of ironic, don't you think?"

"Yes," she answered, looking pensive for a moment as she thought about it. "Life certainly is full of surprises."

Mark got up to clear the table while Darcy and Edward continued to talk. Edward told her he'd found two highly recommended nannies to share the childcare duties, and they would start work the day the baby was born. The due date was only two months away, in early July.

When Mark returned to the table, Edward beamed. "I have one more surprise."

"I'm not sure I can stand any more surprises." Darcy laughed and picked up her coffee cup.

"I spoke to Annie, my surrogate this morning," Edward said sheepishly. "And her ultrasound showed that it's not one baby. It's two. Twin boys!"

Darcy dropped her cup, and coffee splashed everywhere. Mark leaped up to mop up the damage. "Twins?" he repeated aghast. "You're kidding."

"No, I'm not. It's twin boys. Isn't that the most fantastic news you've ever heard?" Edward was ecstatic. Darcy thought she might faint.

"It's pretty unbelievable," Darcy answered slowly. "But truthfully I think it's wonderful. Now the baby won't be an only child and will have a built-in playmate. Being a twin was wonderful for Danielle and me. We were inseparable as kids. Still are. I wish the same special connection for your boys." Tears of happiness began to slide down her cheeks. She understood and cherished the twin bond and had even published a best-selling novel about it several years ago.

"Yes, when you put it like that, I can see it's actually terrific news." Mark nodded. He had marveled at Darcy and Danielle's special relationship over the years. They were so close that they were almost like one person. "And you said you had hired two nannies. You must have had a sixth sense that there was more than one the baby. Have you told Ginger yet?"

"No. I wanted to tell you both first. There's plenty of time."

"Have you thought about any names?" Darcy was curious. She was still reeling from the news.

"Jason and Jackson," Edward announced proudly.

"That couldn't be more perfect," Darcy exclaimed, looking at Mark and Edward. She raised her glass to make a heartfelt toast. "To Jason and Jackson, the twins."

CHAPTER 44

Danielle

Danielle spent most of June working hand in hand with Don and with the senior physicians at New York Hospital to make the mentoring program successful. She made videos of the special lessons she had written geared to medical students' experiences and to those of the interns and residents. She used her powers of persuasion and met with the department heads of the various specialties. She begged, pleaded, and cajoled them into joining the Healing Hands mentoring program.

Then she used her own funds to buy the necessary supplies to implement the expressive writing sessions. Because of her efforts, every medical trainee who was to begin a rotation in July of that year would be included in the mentoring program, and she had secured a senior staff member for each of them. It was a phenomenal achievement, and she received accolades from physicians at other hospitals around the city. Everyone was eager to learn more about Alex's ideas and to participate.

Reducing the high suicide rate among medical students had been one of Alex's motivations, and Danielle hoped that, if even one life was saved, it would be an enormous victory and a lasting tribute to her beloved husband. She still missed him all the time, but keeping his dream alive had helped heal her broken heart and brought her peace. She was still waiting for him to send her the sign of his approval she had requested at his graveside. So far everything remained quiet from "the other side."

Dr. Smith called the board of directors of Healing Words together for a special meeting and proposed that Healing Hands Mentoring become a sister program under their existing corporate umbrella. The concept was unanimously approved, and Danielle received a standing ovation and congratulations from everyone involved. She was thrilled and wished Alex could see what she'd accomplished for his sake. It was a gift of love from her to him … and in some small way, it set her free. She had kept her promise to him by doing something she thought would make him proud. Now she didn't have to be so tied to the past but could look forward to the future.

It had been an arduous month, and Danielle was exhausted but ready to celebrate her achievements. She invited Don and Ray Smith to join her at the Four Seasons for a celebratory dinner, but Dr. Smith begged off. He had a ticket to return to Boston that evening.

"Drink a glass of champagne for me," he said as he kissed Danielle goodbye. "See you soon. Good job, my friend."

"I guess it's just you and me then." Don smiled at her. He was happy to have Danielle to himself for a whole evening with no work involved. "I'll pick you up at seven."

Daniele went home and played with Freddy and Caroline. She had given Lynn the afternoon off, but the nanny was coming back to babysit that evening.

As Danielle was getting dressed for her celebratory dinner out, the phone rang.

"Hi," Darcy said happily. "I miss you. And frankly Mark and I need your help with something here. Do you think you could leave the kids with Lynn and fly down to DC for a weekend? All you've done is work, work, work in the five months since Alex passed, and we think it's time for you to take a break. Connie and Nathan want to see you too, and they've offered you the Lincoln bedroom. How can you turn that down? What do you say?"

"OMG. The Lincoln bedroom?" She was stunned and excited. "That sounds fabulous, but what do you need my help with?"

"I don't mean to be mysterious, but I'd rather wait and tell you in person. It's a little devious."

Danielle couldn't imagine what Darcy meant but was intrigued. "I would love to see everyone down there. Let me talk to Lynn. She's so devoted to the kids. I'm sure she'll be willing to stay with them. Any particular weekend?"

"Connie suggested the Fourth of July. We can watch the fireworks from the balcony off the private living quarters. And," she spoke softly, "it'll be the eighth anniversary of Father's death, and I'd love for us to be together."

"Oh, I'd like that too. With so much going on, I'd forgotten all about the Fourth. This will be a good year for us to get together without my kids because Freddy is still too young for fireworks. The noise would scare him to death. Let me talk to Lynn tonight. She's coming back to babysit in another hour. I'll call you tomorrow with an answer."

"Babysit?" Darcy was curious. "Are you going out … on a date?"

"No, of course not. Don and I are having dinner to celebrate the launching of Healing Hands mentoring. Its official start date is July first."

"Are you sure nothing's going on between you and that nice man? Every time we talk, you are either meeting with him, or he's coming over to help you with the kids."

Darcy truly hoped something was happening between her twin and Don March. He was a nice man and dependable. She felt better knowing he was looking out for Danielle and her children. But Danielle didn't seem to have feelings for him beyond friendship. At least she had never admitted to them. Maybe tonight would change that.

"Nothing's going on." Danielle blushed and switched topics. She wasn't sure how she really felt about Don. He was attractive, smart, and very entertaining, but she didn't have the passionate feelings toward him she'd had for Alex. He made her feel comfortable and safe but not tingly. Maybe at her age and in her circumstances, having someone who cared about and protected her should be enough. She'd already had the great love of her life. Expecting to be struck by lightning a second time was probably unrealistic. And they had never even kissed.

She was also conflicted and felt disloyal to Alex whenever she had any thoughts about another man. Her psychiatrist, Dr. Dorian, claimed those feelings were normal, and she would work through them in time, but she hadn't yet. *Better to ignore them*, she thought. She didn't need any more complications in her life. As it was, she was already pulled in too many different directions.

"Do you still have your red-and-white dress? The one like mine that we've worn on the Fourth for the last few years?" Darcy asked.

"Yes, why?"

"I think it would be fun to continue our tradition of dressing alike. Will you bring it to Washington?"

"Sure. And I'll call you tomorrow about the Fourth." Danielle hung up before Darcy could ask her any more questions about Don March.

CHAPTER 45

Darcy and Danielle

Connie and Darcy happily escorted Danielle into the Lincoln bedroom. It was located in the southeast corner on the second floor of the White House. Furnished in Victorian style, with a soft pastel-yellow printed wallpaper and carpet with an emerald-green, golden-yellow, and deep-purple pattern, the room's centerpiece was the Lincoln bed itself. It was made of Rosewood with an enormous headboard. Legend stated that Lincoln never actually slept in this bed and that during his term as president, the bedroom was used as his personal office. The Emancipation Proclamation was reputed to have been signed there.

"This bedroom is a part of the Lincoln suite," Connie explained to Danielle. "It includes a sitting room and a lovely bathroom. Some of the furnishings are original to Lincoln's time, and some have been added through the years by other administrations. Recently it's been used as a guest room for special people like you, my dear friend, and for important, high-rolling political donors."

"Well, I'm beyond thrilled," Danielle said enthusiastically as she looked around the historic room. "What a treat to be here and especially to be with you and Darcy."

"Just to warn you." Connie smiled mischievously. "This bedroom is supposed to be haunted. Over the years, a few guests have reported seeing ghosts in here."

"Nothing brightens up the evening like a friendly ghost." Danielle laughed. "May I see more of your living quarters and where Darcy works?"

"Sure, I'll lead the way, and later Nathan will show you the Oval Office."

Connie instructed the butler to unpack Danielle's belonging and then led Danielle and Darcy on a tour through the White House public and private rooms and over to the East Wing. After the tour, they returned to the sun-filled sitting room the Pierces used as their living room. Over tall glasses of mint iced tea and egg-salad sandwiches, the three friends spent the next few hours chatting and catching up.

"Politics is off limits for the moment," Connie announced. She turned toward Danielle. "I want to hear all about your life in New York and the children. Are you really as okay as you seem?"

"Yes, I am, surprisingly so." Danielle sipped her drink. "When Alex died, I thought I couldn't live any longer. I had no idea how to raise two children on my own. Thankfully I have a wonderful support group including Darcy, Ray Smith, Don March, and my new psychiatrist, Dr. Dorian. Because of them and my good friends, like you, Connie, I don't like it, but I've accepted what happened and decided that I have to make a good life for myself and for Freddy and Caroline. To do less would dishonor Alex's memory. Now every time I want to do something new, I ask myself, *What would Alex think?* If the answer is, *He'd be proud of me*, I go for it. If I'm not sure, I put it off for another time."

"That sounds reasonable." Darcy grinned. "But now that it's just us girls here, tell us about the intriguing and quite-devoted Dr. Don March."

Danielle twisted uncomfortably in her chair. She didn't like discussing her personal life. "I can't give you an honest answer. I vacillate. Sometimes I think I might be attracted to him and that I'd like to have a more personal relationship. But at other times I know he's not Alex, and I will never feel about him the way I did about my husband." She rolled her wedding ring nervously around her finger. "It may sound silly, but as long as I'm wearing Alex's ring, I'm still committed to him."

"I understand. There's no rush," Connie said in support. "It's only been five months. You'll know when the time is right to take off your ring. And even when you do, remember you won't be discarding Alex. It will only be a sign that you are adjusted to your new reality and are ready to move on. We never forget the ones we've loved, but gradually they lose their tight hold on us."

"I know you're right," Darcy agreed. "I'm just tired of seeing Danielle depressed. I want her to be happy again ... I mean, really happy, like she used to be."

"You'll be the first to know." Danielle winked at her sister. "And on another note, I can't believe Father died eight years ago today. In many ways it seems like a lifetime ago and yet just yesterday. I vividly remember every detail of that last night."

"He died right after you all watched the fireworks together from his home in New York, didn't he?" Connie remembered the touching story.

"Yes. He was so happy that he finally had his girls back together. He died knowing we all loved each other," Darcy said in an emotional tone. "His was a sad and touching passing, and it came way too soon."

"Have you heard anything from Karin?" Connie asked. She remembered how cruel their stepmother had been to Danielle and Darcy in their youth. Karin had caused the separation of the twins, which took fifteen years to mend, and she was responsible for their prolonged alienation from their father.

"Thank goodness, I haven't seen or heard from the witch since Bill Robinson informed her that she was virtually penniless. Bless my father's heart. He got revenge for all of us with the provisions he put in his will." Danielle frowned. "I know it's not politically correct to admit, but that was a wonderfully satisfying moment for Darcy and me. The look on her plastic-surgery-enhanced face was priceless when she learned she was flat broke and would have to get a job."

"Yes, it was," Darcy agreed. "And come to think of it, I remember Bill Robinson left Mark a message a while ago. I think he mentioned Karin's name, but I don't believe the two ever connected. Remind me to ask Mark about it later."

"Much later." Danielle grimaced. "Let's not let Karin ruin this wonderful Fourth of July. Can we go see the Oval now?"

"In just a minute." Connie looked at Darcy conspiratorially. "Darcy and I want to talk to you about a plan we've made. You've got to swear to keep it a secret."

Darcy and Connie told Danielle about the vicious and persistent leaks coming from someone in the White House and how they were affecting Mark's credibility with the press corps and Nathan's ability to get his agenda through Congress. Of late, the leaks had become increasingly more personal, not only attacking Nathan's presidency but also his marriage and making innuendos about Nathan's fidelity, likening him to a philandering Bill Clinton. They insinuated that he was having an affair with a top-level staffer in the White House and named Darcy as the likely lover. The situation was worsening day by day as the tabloids fed on and perpetuated the untrue rumors. Nathan's popularity in the polls was plummeting. Mark had to spend most of his time dispelling the rumors, and Connie and Danielle were enraged and wanted to do something about them.

"We're going to fix this mess." Darcy leaned closer to her sister. They had to be very careful, even in the private quarters. They didn't know whether anyone was watching or recording them. Someone on the White House staff was disloyal and undermining Nathan. They were determined to find out who.

CHAPTER 46

Darcy

Darcy and Mark left the White House and went home to change for their dinner later that evening in the private quarters with Nathan, Connie, and Danielle. They planned to watch the fireworks together afterward.

Darcy loved being with Danielle again. As much as she loved her job, she missed the daily contact with her sister, and having Danielle around reminded her of what she had sacrificed to move back to DC. Freddy was getting bigger every day, and Caroline didn't even know her. She was beginning to second-guess their decision to move. Had she and Mark agreed to take their new jobs at the White House so quickly because they were so distraught about their sudden firing from ESPN? She was no longer sure.

"Darling," she casually said to Mark as he put on a pair of navy blue linen slacks and a patriotic red, white, and blue top. "Remember when Bill Robinson called and said he wanted to speak to you. Did you ever talk to him?"

"No, damn it. I didn't. I'm sorry. I got so caught up in our move and the new job and your breast," he said, smiling at her affectionately, "that I completely forgot."

"We don't have to leave for a little while yet. Why don't you try to reach him now? I have his cell number in my contacts."

"On a holiday?"

"Sure, why not? He's the one who called you first. I'm sure he won't mind."

"Okay." Mark put on his navy sports jacket and carefully placed a red handkerchief in the front pocket. He took Darcy's phone. "Hi, Bill. Sorry to bother you on a holiday," he began. "It's Mark. Are you free to talk for a minute?" He walked into his home office and shut the door. "I'm sorry I never called you back. Things have been pretty hectic around here."

"Of course, I understand. It's nice to hear from you. I've been thinking about you and your family. I know this is the anniversary of Fred Coulter's death. He was a good friend to me, and I still miss him."

"We all do, Bill. Thank you for that. You left us a message a while ago?"

"Yes, I did. I wanted to give you an update on the ESPN situation."

"Did you find out who accused me and of what precisely?"

"Not quite, but I'm getting close. I hired a private investigator to poke around. He's been talking to people at ESPN. Two of them reported that you were less than truthful on air and that you often exaggerated stories and planted fake clues to jack up your ratings."

Mark was speechless. "That never happened," he shouted angrily.

Mr. Robinson continued. "This unnamed accuser took her complaints to management, claiming your actions would damage and forever taint ESPN's reputation. She brought a witness along to back up her story. They both claimed to have been standing outside your office door and overheard you admit to someone that the major league baseball story you had just broken about cheating in the World Series wasn't completely accurate and that you were hoping the story would get legs of its own and generate another scandal like the University of Maryland basketball story did for your career a few years ago. The network lawyers considered the accusations very seriously and thoroughly questioned the two witnesses. They then recorded their testimony, and those depositions became the basis for your dismissal under the guise of failing to live up to the morals clause in your contract."

"But that *never* happened," Mark protested vehemently. "I've never gone on air without proper fact-checking. At the time, I didn't know the full extent of the MLB cheating and its ramifications, but I reported that the Astros would be reporting to training camp under a huge black cloud. Soon the team would be found guilty of using an electronic sign-stealing scheme throughout their season and into the playoffs. This cheating helped them win games and advance to the World Series. That's one hundred percent accurate, and I stand by my story. It was proven to be true and was reported in all the papers just recently. At the time, however, I was protecting my source. I didn't want to name names until the official investigation was concluded. I knew it was about to become the greatest cheating scandal since the Black Sox in 1919."

"This whole thing was a vicious setup. I'm just repeating the information I was given. Don't shoot the messenger, please. I can tell you that after what happened in the television industry in recent years, ESPN wasn't interested in dragging their company's good name through the mud with a prolonged investigation into your behavior. Remember, to this day NBC still has not recovered from the Matt Lauer fiasco.

"The network clearly decided to pay off the accusers and cut its losses. They offered the witnesses a financial settlement on the condition that they sign nondisclosure agreements and agree never to discuss the situation or the settlement again. I thought I had tracked down one of the two witnesses, but it turned out to be a dead end. The investigator is continuing to look. We will find them."

"Can't we at least get our hands on the depositions?" Mark asked. "Surely I have that right?"

"The depositions are sealed and locked in the lawyer's vault. Unfortunately, you are not entitled to see them, as you were supposedly fired for cause ... for breaching the ethic clause of your contract. The two 'convenient' witnesses provided sworn evidence of your guilt and claimed that they were afraid of reprisal from you too, so the network is protecting them. It's a 'they-said/you-said' situation."

"I can't believe this. It's totally unfair! There's *no* proof because it never happened! No one could have overheard anything." Mark shook his head at the absurdity of it all. "I've been totally railroaded, my reputation ruined, and my livelihood compromised by lies ... despicable lies! Do you have any idea who orchestrated this?"

"The source described the woman witness in vivid detail. He was quite specific. From the description he gave the PI, I believe he described a woman who looked and acted a great deal like Darcy's stepmother, Karin. He specifically mentioned the bright-red nail polish that Karin favored and that the woman wore distinctive pearl and diamond dangling earring. I remember your father gave Karin a pair matching that description as a wedding present. We need to get a photo of Karin, hopefully wearing those earrings, and give it to the private investigator. Do you have one?"

"I don't know. I'll look for one. Maybe in an old album somewhere. Certainly not on display. We never wanted to see Karin again after everything she'd done to Fred, Darcy, and Danielle." Mark lowered his voice. "I need time to process all this. For now, let's keep this between us men. I don't want to bring Karin back into Darcy's life unless I have to or until we have definite proof that she was involved in my firing."

"Understood. I'll keep in touch. But get me a picture ASAP." Mark said his goodbyes and hung up. He went straight to his bar and poured a very stiff scotch.

CHAPTER 47

Danielle and Darcy

Danielle was thrilled to be staying in the White House and spending the Fourth of July holiday with her close friends. She wished Alex could have been with them. He had been such a fan of Nathan's and would have loved to be part of all the pomp and circumstance in the White House on the nation's birthday. She also loved being with Darcy and Mark. The experience made her feel like old times when they had all spent so much time together in New York. She missed those times almost as much as she missed Alex.

Danielle enjoyed the rest of the tour, including the Oval Office, the state dining room, and the red and blue rooms. The White House was much smaller in size than she had realized … nothing compared to Buckingham Palace or the Kremlin. But to her, it was magical and cozy, and she felt privileged being there.

"Did you run into any ghosts while you were changing?" Connie asked Danielle in jest as they gathered for drinks before dinner and the fireworks.

"None that I could see, but the bedroom curtains did shimmy slightly."

"That's because the air-conditioning vents blow directly on them." Connie laughed. "As long as you didn't hear voices, I think you're safe."

Mark took his wine glass and strolled over to the large window to join everyone else looking out at the Washington Monument and across the mall. "I had the most enlightening conversation with Bill Robinson right before Darcy and I came back here tonight."

"Oh." Nathan was intrigued. "What did he have to say?"

"Well, first, he remembered that tonight is the anniversary of Fred Coulter's death, and he told me how much he missed his old friend."

"That was nice." Danielle smiled sadly. "I miss my father too. He would have loved to be here tonight with all of us."

"Then," Mark continued, not wanting Danielle's nostalgia to distract him, "he went on to explain that he'd hired a detective to find out the truth about what went on at ESPN … why I was fired. He said that a mysterious woman had come forth and accused me of lying and exaggerating stories on air. She brought in a witness to collaborate her story, and the two gave depositions to the network lawyers."

"Can you imagine?" Darcy added bitterly. Mark had told her about his conversation with Mr. Robinson but omitted the part about Karin. "Someone was out to get Mark, but why? For what? He had no enemies that we know of. I can't figure out who would want to hurt him so badly."

Mark didn't want to ruin the evening, so he didn't mention Mr. Robinson's theory that Karin was the possible culprit. He vowed to himself that as soon as he got home, he'd find a picture of Karin somewhere and get it to his lawyer in the morning. Until then Karin was as good as dead to him and the family.

"To Fred Coulter, a fine gentleman and a loving father." Mark raised his glass to his deceased father-in-law.

"To Daddy," Danielle and Darcy echoed and clinked their crystal flutes.

Connie looked at her husband and her dear friends. "Thanks, everyone," she said, smiling warmly, "for agreeing to help with Darcy's plan. After we're done tomorrow, I hope the rumors will stop and it will be a brighter day for us all."

"Here, here." Danielle winked at her sister. "Just like old times."

The firework display began, and they moved out onto the balcony to watch the spectacular show.

CHAPTER 48

The Press Briefing

Early the next morning, Connie led Danielle and Darcy down the back steps from the private quarters and quietly through the hallways to the Oval Office. The White House staff had been hard at work for hours and weren't paying attention to the First Lady's comings and goings. The president was meeting with his cabinet, so his office was deserted. Connie nodded good morning to Nathan's secretary and ushered the twins inside.

"Now what?" Danielle asked. "How will this play out?"

"Last night Mark orchestrated today's presentation," Darcy replied. "Turn to the national CBS news and just watch. At the top of the hour, they will be running a derogatory piece about Nathan and his supposed sexual antics with Darcy. Mark will be watching it with the White House press corps at the same time."

The three women sat tensely on the sofa and stared expectantly at the television screen. A familiar male reporter was shown standing on the White House lawn with his mic in hand. His body language reflected a sober announcement, but his gleeful, snickering facial expression suggested otherwise.

"Yesterday," the reporter began, "the president of the United States was enjoying the day off for the Fourth of July holiday with close friends, but today he can expect some internal fireworks in his own household. This reporter has uncovered a tape … which I am going to play for you now ... proving an ongoing affair between the president and his press secretary's wife, the beautiful and beguiling Darcy Donavan. As the video will show, the two have been constantly photographed together, carrying on in the Oval Office, on Air Force One, and elsewhere. In complete denial, the First Lady continues to ignore the evidence, calling the rumors ridiculous, but here is the undeniable truth. It is as damning as Monica's blue dress."

The reporter began the tape with the first frame showing the president and Darcy going in and out of the Oval together, laughing and talking intimately. The president's left hand could clearly be seen patting and caressing Darcy's buttock as they entered the office and swiftly closed the door. The next frame revealed Darcy and the president leaving the office. This time the president's arm was around her waist, and he appeared to be nibbling on her neck. There were two more such frames, each showing the president and Darcy engaged in some sort of physical contact.

"These tapes were taken by the White House security cameras over the last few months," he stated officiously. "They demonstrate an obvious intimate relationship the president can no longer deny and the First Lady can no longer ignore. I contend that this indisputable, outrageous behavior, reminiscent of Bill Clinton and his sexual antics, renders Nathan Pierce unfit to remain in office."

The crowd in the press room stirred uneasily and started to mumble among themselves. Everyone looked toward the podium as Mark took his place for his regular briefing.

"Ladies and gentlemen—and I use those words loosely." He had to shout to make himself heard over the noise of their chatter. "I am sick and tired of the innuendos and false rumors concerning the president and my wife. I am here today to put an end to these scurrilous lies and to hold the responsible party accountable."

Suddenly, the room became very still. All eyes were on the beleaguered press secretary. Mark was prepared. He and Darcy had been up most of the night, rehearsing what he was going to say and consulting with a friend at the FBI. What Mark was about to do was a definite gamble, but he believed that showing the truth was worth the risk of alienating the press corps. They wouldn't like being made to look foolish, but it was necessary to restore decorum to the White House. Nathan and Connie were in complete agreement. Mark knew he would either be believed now, or the press corps would hound the president to fire him.

He lowered the overhead lights and said, "I have a big advantage over you members of the press, because over the decades of my sports broadcasting career, I have watched literally thousands of video replay tapes. I have learned to search for miniscule lines of evidence. For example, in a football game, in instant replay, did the receiver's foot come down in bounds? Or did his knee hit the ground before the ball came loose?" Ninety percent of the reporters in the room nodded their heads in agreement. They understood the football analogy.

"This video was made last night to prove my point," Mark announced solemnly. "It shows President Pierce entering the Oval Office, with his arm supposedly around Darcy, and closing the door. A few minutes later, Darcy appears to come out alone. Shortly thereafter, the president comes out and brings Darcy back into the room. This sequence is repeated several times, and each time President Pierce is seen touching Darcy's arm or buttocks, or holding her hand. The last frame in this video shows the Oval Office door slowly opening and the president walking out proudly with his right arm around Darcy and his left arm around her identical twin sister, Danielle."

The crowd gasped. Many hadn't realized that Darcy Donavan was a twin. They had been fooled by a doctored tape and certainly had no way of knowing two different women were in the same video ... going in and out of the Oval Office.

Mark explained to the crowd that his wife always wore a thin golden bracelet with a heart-shaped charm engraved with "D & D" for Donavan & Donavan, and Danielle always wore a delicate pearl ring her father had given her right before he died. When Mark froze the video frames, it was easy for him to point out which girl was which because of their jewelry.

"Pictures and videos can be deceiving," he stated soberly. "They can be made and then edited to suggest untruths. They can be maliciously fabricated by someone with a personal agenda. You, the public, see exactly what you've been conditioned to see and believe what you've been told to believe. In the case of the video of the president and my wife, shown to us by your colleague a few minutes ago, he has deliberately distorted and photoshopped the images. They appear to suggest the garbage that you have been spoon fed. You want to believe the worst about our president, so you do. You, ladies and gentleman of the press, have been victims of your own 'fake news.' And thankfully, with the help of Agent Fosterer from the FBI, who taught me how to uncover a fraudulent video, I will now play back that tape and show you exactly where it was doctored.

"First, please see the small lapse of time when the president puts his hand on my wife's buttocks. The frame jumps a fraction. That signals that something was added or deleted. Also note that the president is wearing no jewelry on his left hand. Nathan Perce always wears his wedding ring. There is not one picture of him taken since his marriage when that ring is not on his finger. Also check out the size of the president's head. It's a little bigger than normal and out of proportion with his body. That's because it is not the president in this video but a clever photoshopped impersonation, deliberately inserted to mislead you. In addition, if you look closely, you will see that the American flag pin the president always wears on his lapel is missing."

No one in the room dared to breathe. Mark had them almost hypnotized.

"In the last election, President Pierce wasn't the media's choice, although he was duly elected by the American public. So therefore, everything about him, his polices and initiatives, his choice of meat versus vegetables, and his relationships with his coworkers and friends is suspect. You use whatever you can, true or not, to discredit him, and you should be ashamed.

"That's what's wrong with our country today. Nobody gets the benefit of the doubt anymore. A person is no longer considered innocent before being proven guilty. Just the opposite. Now after looking at those tapes and seeing how the truth can so easily be distorted, do you still think our president is having an affair with my wife? If so, I dare you to point Darcy out—without looking at her jewelry, that is." There was nervous laughter from the crowd. "Was she alone with the president in the Oval Office as the tape seems to indicate, or was her sister there too?

Or was he engaged in hanky-panky with both of them? Or—more to the point—with *neither* of them?

"In this case," Mark continued, "you, and by extension the American public, have been manipulated by a devious reporter from the *National Intrigue*. You all know him, Gregg Matlok, your colleague, who has his own agenda, which is to defame our president and ignite an impeachment process." Mark spoke directly to the shameless man. "Mr. Matlok, would you like to retract your accusations and publicly apologize to my wife, to the president of the United States, and to the First Lady?"

The disgraced reported angrily threw his iPad on the floor in fury and stormed out of the room. The press corps was stunned. The twins had pulled off another switch, just like they used to do as kids. As children, it had been fun, an adventure to see whether they could fool their teachers or parents. But in this one, the stakes had been much higher. Darcy and Danielle's switch had been intended to restore Nathan and Darcy's reputations and cast doubt on any future unfounded stories. Mark hoped the press would learn from this and more meticulously fact-check everything before printing a story.

Mark walked off the podium and over to Darcy and Danielle, who had entered from the back of the room. He hugged them both as dozens of flashbulbs clicked to record the victorious moment. One by one the reporters stood up, clapping loudly until the entire room was giving Mark a standing ovation. In the Oval Office, President Pierce smiled broadly at the First Lady. He had been vindicated.

CHAPTER 49

Danielle

Danielle returned to New York after a wonderful weekend in Washington. She'd had the time of her life pulling off the switch on the White House press corps. It was like old times in boarding school with Darcy. She had laughed the whole day and enjoyed watching the various reporters on the White House beat come up and apologize to Nathan and Connie. It had been rewarding for once to see the good guys win. There would probably be more rumors and false news in the future, but for the moment, everything was good, and hopefully Nathan and his administration could get on with the business of running the government. She had been so proud of Mark and his fiery speech. She wished Alex could have heard it.

Danielle was thrilled to see her children again. She spent the afternoon playing games with them and cooking Freddy's favorite meal for supper. When she was finished unpacking, she gave Freddy some souvenirs from the White House and Caroline a toy Connie and Nathan had sent for her.

Danielle was proud of herself for having left the children with Lynn. She had called only once a day to check on them, although she'd been tempted to reach out more frequently. After Alex's death, she was haunted that something terrible would happen to her family. But she was trying to fight the fear.

In the last five months, she had come a long way in her journey of self-discovery with Dr. Dorian's help. She had conquered many of her fears and truly believed that being Dr. Danielle Stone was enough. She had nothing to prove to anyone, no mountains to climb. She was a whole person, flawed but strong and loving. Danielle accepted that she would always be too cautious, a little afraid to take risks, and maybe a little overprotective of her children. That was her nature. She had gained personal insight and believed she was brave enough to press forward alone and provide a good life for herself and her children. She had Ray Smith and Dr. Dorian to thank for that.

"How was the weekend in DC?" Dr. Dorian asked in their next session.

"Very nice. Wonderful, in fact." Danielle beamed. "It was terrific being with Darcy and the Pierces. And sleeping in the Lincoln bedroom … words can't describe the thrill of that."

"How did you feel about the Fourth of July, it being the anniversary of your father's death? Did that memory dredge up dark thoughts or fears?"

Danielle thought for a moment before answering, "No, not really. We spoke about Father and shared stories about him with humor and love. Everything was fine … surprisingly so."

She went on to describe that they had all gone to the Oval in the middle of the night to make the tape that brought the sleezy tabloid reporter down and squashed the infidelity rumors once and for all. She was proud of her part in it. And she couldn't wait to end the therapy session and get to work to tell Don all about it. She was surprised to realize how much she wanted to share the experience with him and how much she'd missed seeing him.

CHAPTER 50

Darcy

Darcy was sad after Danielle returned to her life in New York City. Her absence left a big void, impossible to fill. It was the "twin thing." However, she understood that she was being selfish. Danielle's Healing Words business; Alex's new mentoring program, Healing Hands; and her children were all in New York. Darcy couldn't expect her sister to stop everything and move to DC. So she resolved to focus on the things she could accomplish besides doing her job as Connie's personal assistant.

Mark had finally confided in her about Mr. Robinson's suspicions that Karin was somehow involved in Mark's firing. Darcy had stewed about the matter ever since, and she felt compelled to locate Karin and find out if there was any truth to it.

But where to begin?

Darcy wasn't sure what to do, so she called Bill Robinson to ask him the name of the private investigator who had spoken to the people at ESPN. Bill was out of the country on business, but his secretary gladly provided the name and address of the PI firm and the name of the person he'd dealt with there. Darcy called and made a phone appointment for herself to speak to him the next morning.

"Sorry to interrupt." Connie strolled into Darcy's office, smiling broadly. "I have good news. Edward's twin boys were born last night at Fairfax Hospital. They are both healthy, seven pounds plus, with all their fingers and toes. Edward is ecstatic, and Ginger is over the moon. He and the two nannies are bringing the babies home later today. Ginger and Lloyd are going over to Edward's place to meet them. Ginger can't wait to cuddle those little munchkins. I've never heard her sound so happy. She was actually bubbling when she called me with the news.

"Nathan wants to give them all a little time to settle in and then visit his baby nephews this evening. Would you and Mark like to come along? We can sneak out of here and drop by Edward's for a couple of minutes."

"Sure. That would be great. We have little silver cups to give the babies. I had Tiffany's engrave their names on them. Of course, I know they'll never use them, but they'll look cute on a shelf somewhere. I'll run home at lunchtime and get them. Then we'll be ready to leave whenever you say."

"I'll alert the secret service so they'll be prepared." Connie turned to leave. "By the way, I can't thank you and Danielle enough for making that video. The press has been much kinder to Nathan since then."

"De nada." Darcy giggled. "Switching places with each other is one of the many benefits of being a twin. Edward is going to experience that now that the little guys are here."

CHAPTER 51

Danielle

Danielle was working at home. Freddy had a slight fever and a sore throat. She didn't want to go to the office when he wasn't feeling well. He was lying quietly on the sofa, watching a Disney movie. Danielle was going through a stack of mail the office had sent over as well as her own personal bills. She had fallen behind on her paperwork, so she needed this day to go through everything and catch up. She wasn't like Darcy, who compulsively had to check everything off her to-do list every night before bedtime, but she wasn't one for excessive clutter or unfinished business either. She sat with her checkbook in front of her and her online banking site open on her computer screen.

When she finished paying the bills for Healing Words and Healing Hands, she answered e-mails and read through several financial reports. The fiscal year for the two programs had just ended, and she wanted to be on top of the projections for the next quarter. She needed to know how much of her personal money she'd have to contribute to keep the programs going for another year. Hers was a nonprofit organization, which relied solely on her funds and donations to sustain itself.

Lynn brought Freddy a grilled cheese sandwich and a bowl of tomato soup. He ate in front of the television, still happily engrossed in his movie. Lynn fed Caroline in the kitchen because she was such a messy eater, and she threw food everywhere. Danielle skipped lunch to continue working while the children were fairly quiet.

She finished paying the household bills and picked up a large manila envelope hidden in a stack of magazines and medical journals. The journals accumulated so fast she could barely keep up with them. She hadn't canceled any of Alex's, and she also had to read her own.

Danielle didn't recognize the return address. It was from someplace in the city. After tearing open the envelope, she pulled out a letter and started to read.

> Dear Dr. Stone,
>
> I am the producer of the Nettime's television series *Real People*. Perhaps you have heard of it? It's the number one-rated reality show in America right now.
>
> My company is aware of your program, Healing Words, and what it has done for cancer patients. I would like to discuss the possibility of filming you and focusing on your expressive writing program for our spring lineup. This would entail extensive interviews with you, your patients, and your staff. I would film various sessions you conduct and then follow up with certain patients a year later to see how they have done medically.
>
> As I'm sure you know, *Real People* is a very popular show, and the publicity our show generates would be beneficial to your endeavors and probably generate large donations to your cause.
>
> I would like to set up a personal meeting with you to discuss this matter further. Please call my office at 917-555-1515 as soon as possible for an appointment.
>
> Sincerely, William Bell

Danielle was flabbergasted. She loved *Real People* and was a regular viewer. Alex had loved the show too. They had made it a point to tape it and watch it together each week. The topics were far ranging and interesting, and the show explored their subjects in great depth. She had never thought that Healing Words would be of interest to their audience, but the more she thought about it, the more she realized this might be good fit and the chance of a lifetime. Maybe she could introduce Alex's mentoring program too. A win for her and a win for Alex.

She was so excited that she called Darcy right away before she even put the letter down. Her sister's phone went right to voice mail, so Danielle dialed Don instead. "Guess what?" she began ecstatically, not waiting for him to say hello. "Things are about to change around here. I'm going to be a television star."

"What do you mean?" He could hear the excitement in her voice. He loved it when she was happy.

"I just opened the mail that's been sitting on my desk since I was in DC. There's a letter from one of the producers of *Real People*, the reality television show. He wants to talk to me about the possibility of doing a series of shows on our Healing Words program. It would be such wonderful publicity for us. What do you think?"

"I think it sounds fabulous. By all means talk to him. You'll make a wonderful spokesperson and a great face for the program—and a damn pretty one at that." She could almost see his grin through the phone. "Let me take you out to dinner tonight to celebrate."

"Truthfully, I'd rather stay home, Don. Freddy has a bit of a temperature and a little sore throat. I've got stroganoff in the freezer and the makings for a salad. Why don't you come here instead?"

"You're on. That'll be fine. What's the name of the producer? I'll see what I can find out about him before I come over this evening."

"The letter was signed by William Bell."

"Okay. I'll dig around a little. You might also want to call Darcy and Mark. With their television connections, they might know or have heard of him. Just to be sure he's legit."

"I've already tried to reach Darcy but couldn't. I'll call her again in a little while. In the meantime, I'll make an appointment to meet with Mr. Bell as soon as possible."

"One word of caution," he warned. "Be sure to talk to the company and the hospital lawyers before you sign anything. They may have privacy and patients' rights issues."

"Yes, of course." She had already thought about those. Why did men always assume a woman couldn't think for herself? She quickly hung up on Don, impatient to reach Mr. Bell before his office closed for the day.

CHAPTER 52

Darcy

Darcy was anxious to talk to Tony Gantz, the private eye Mr. Robinson had hired previously. She had scanned him a copy of her father's will along with some old photos of Karin Coulter taken at a charity event and at parties around New York. In one she was wearing the earrings Fred had given her as a wedding present.

When Darcy spoke with Mr. Gantz, she told him the unvarnished truth about her stepmother. She explained that at the time of Fred Coulter's death, Karin could barely tolerate her husband and had for years surrounded herself with lovers. She was disillusioned with her marriage and had begged Fred for a divorce. He steadfastly refused ... not because he still loved his cheating, greedy wife but because he wanted to make her suffer for what she had done to alienate him from his daughters.

Fred Coulter had been a nice man, but he'd been altogether too human. Forgiveness didn't come easily. He wanted revenge for all the pain Karin had caused him and his twins. She and Brett Fletcher, one of her many lovers, had swindled Fred out of the majority of his fortune and publicly humiliated him. Fred never forgave the two, not because of his financial losses, which over time he was able to recoup, but because of the painful fifteen-year estrangement Karin's schemes and behaviors had caused between him and his daughters.

Darcy talked extensively with the private investigator and told him everything she could about Karin, her habits, her few friends, her lovers, and especially Brett Fletcher. Then she explained that in the end, her father had gotten his justice by leaving Karin penniless in his will. She reiterated that she and Danielle hadn't seen or heard from Karin since Bill Robinson read them all the provisions of Fred's will eight years ago.

"That's quite a story," Tony Gantz said. "This Karin dame seems like a real bitch."

"That she is," Darcy readily agreed. "And I want to confront her personally if you can find her."

"I'll do my best," he replied. "And I'll take these photos to my source at ESPN and see if he can identify her. If so, that's all the proof we need."

After agreeing on a fee, Darcy hung up with a feeling of hope. She liked Tony Gantz and felt he was competent and experienced, and that he was going to be able to track Karin down. Then she and Mark would take it from there.

CHAPTER 53

Danielle

Danielle had met with William Bell, the producer of *Real People* shows, numerous times in the last month and had conferred with the lawyers of the Healing Words program and the New York Hospital. After several weeks of negotiating, the legal papers were signed by all parties, and shooting was scheduled to begin.

The first scene was to be shot in Danielle's former office, and then the cameras would move to the hospital site. There would be eight weekly episodes, and at the end of the last episode, Dan March would be introduced as the new executive officer of the program, and he would make the final comments to close the series. Anticipation was high, and a possible Emmy nomination was rumored.

Danielle loved the excitement of being involved in a television series, especially her meetings with William Bell. She hadn't enjoyed this kind of male comradery since Alex. William was a confirmed bachelor in his midfifties. He was handsome with salt-and-pepper hair, and he had a dimple in the middle of his chin. His personality was infectious, and he had a keen, discerning eye for detail. Nothing got past him. He ruled the set with an iron fist but fairly and with humor. The crew admired and loved him. Sometimes Danielle wondered whether she was falling for him too.

William was equally as taken with Danielle. He was fascinated by how she'd come up with the idea for the program and how she'd taken it from a fledgling writing program in the chemo wing of one hospital to an astounding, successful, expressive writing program that had spread nationwide and was helping thousands of cancer and seriously ill patients. He found Danielle exciting, and he couldn't spend enough time with her. Sometimes he made up excuses to hold one more meeting or film one more take just so she wouldn't leave and go home.

William was also intrigued with Danielle herself. He was a confirmed bachelor in his early fifties, a true ladies' man. He found her astonishingly beautiful, and he admired her spunk and that she'd survived the sudden loss of her husband and that she was raising her two small children alone. He had always been a player but wondered if maybe Danielle was the one woman who could tame him.

From their many conversations, he knew she'd not always been so strong, but with the help of caring psychiatrists, she had come to terms with her life and accepted it. He wasn't sure he would have been able to if he'd been in her place. He had tried to ask her out on dates, but she always pleaded needing to be at home with her children. She didn't seem to want or need a man in her life. She often said that Alex had been so wonderful that she couldn't imagine anyone ever taking his place.

Don was jealous of the time Danielle and William spent together. Every time he saw them, they were laughing or huddled together, discussing some important matter. In a few short weeks, he had gone from being Danielle's sounding board, best friend, and right-hand man to a simple bystander. He felt like a groupie, and he resented it. Danielle hadn't meant for him to feel that way, but she didn't have the time to constantly reassure him and include him in the production meetings and endless script revisions. William Bell was deliberately keeping her too busy.

Danielle was pulled in too many different directions, and for the moment, besides her children, William and making the *Real People* shows were her priorities. She had been working around the clock, perfecting her acting abilities and seamlessly memorizing her dialogue. The entire television crew had fallen in love with her and held her in great esteem. But they could see, as did William and Don, that the last hectic weeks had taken a toll on Danielle's health. She was losing weight because she never took the time to eat, and she was always tired. She used her children as the excuse, claiming they were running her ragged. She never begged off work and was the first person on the set in the mornings and the last to leave in the evenings.

After episode four was wrapped up, she developed a hacking cough and found it hard to finish a scene without stopping numerous times to gargle or gulp down Robitussin. William gave her some lemon cough drops and medicine with codeine, but they didn't help. She continued to cough, sometimes so hard that she thought she'd cracked a rib. She didn't go to a doctor for an X-ray in case he forbade her to work. She had to finish the series.

Danielle was panicked that if she called in sick, she would be responsible for shutting down the production, and the Healing Words segments would be replaced by something different; then the program would never be resurrected. William had often told her what a cutthroat business television was and that as important and influential as he was, another scrappy producer would always be waiting to pounce on the opportunity to knock him down and promote their own story ideas. There would always be a new idea for a new show and a new star waiting to be discovered. That was the way of the entertainment business.

Danielle worried that if she took a few sick days off, the show might be canceled before the first episode was broadcast, and all her efforts and hard work would go to waste. Healing Words wouldn't get the exposure, and she wouldn't have the chance to introduce Alex's Healing Hands mentoring program. The heavy responsibility for both programs depended on her ability to perform and finish the series. When Danielle felt uncertain or threatened, she did what she always had done. She called Darcy.

CHAPTER 54

Darcy

Darcy arrived at Danielle's apartment the morning after Danielle had called her. It was mid-September, and the crisp New York air signaled the arrival of fall.

"I forget the difference in temperatures between DC and New York. It can be steamy in Washington and downright chilly here," Darcy said as she removed her blazer and went over to hug her sister. She was shocked by how ill Danielle looked. "You look god awful, if you don't mind me saying so. I'm taking you to a doctor right this minute. Get a sweater or jacket and come with me."

Danielle started to protest but started a coughing fit and was helpless to stop Darcy from literally shoving her out the door. "Lynn," Darcy called out to the nanny, "I'm taking Danielle to the doctor. Please watch the kids, and we'll be back as soon as we can."

Four hours later, Darcy returned to the condo by herself. Danielle had been diagnosed with pneumonia and admitted to the hospital for treatment.

"Mommy's sick, and the doctor wants her to spend a day or two in the hospital so they can take care of her," Darcy gently explained to Freddy and Caroline. "But don't worry. I'll be here, and so will Lynn."

"Can we get her some cherry popsicles?" Freddy asked soberly. "That's what Mommy always gives me when I'm sick."

"What a good idea," Darcy answered and hugged the little boy tenderly. "Maybe tomorrow."

Lynn could tell Darcy wanted to speak to her privately, so she led the children into their playroom and set out a puzzle for them. "I want to talk to your aunt Darcy, and then I'll come back and help you. Okay?" she said to the children.

Freddy and Caroline were already busy moving the large wooden pieces around and paid no attention to her. Lynn smiled at their concentration. Danielle was doing an excellent job raising them. They were such great kids.

"Danielle is quite sick," Darcy explained to the nanny. "But after the antibiotics kick in, she should feel much better. She'll most likely be in the hospital for three or four days. She has pneumonia. In the meantime, she doesn't want anyone to know where she is. Not anyone. Do you understand?"

"Sure." Lynn was puzzled but promised not to say a word. "Not even Dr. March? But what about Mr. Bell and the television show? She's supposed to start filming episode five tomorrow morning. The script is on her desk in her bedroom."

"I'll handle that," Darcy answered. "Just keep your promise, and if anyone calls, tell them she's out and offer to take a message, please."

"Will you be staying here or upstairs in your place?"

"I'll sleep in Danielle's room so I can spend some time with the children. I'll be here until Danielle gets home and feels strong enough to go back to work."

Darcy walked into Danielle's bedroom, closed the door, and picked up the *Real People* script. She had a lot to memorize by morning.

CHAPTER 55

Danielle

Danielle was furious. She had allowed herself to get run down, and now she had pneumonia to show for her stupidity. The doctor assured her that after she finished the course of intravenous antibiotics in the hospital and had a few days of rest at home, she'd be able to go back to filming the show. That meant Darcy would have to cover for her for at least a week on the set, in production meetings, while she worked with the script rewrites; most importantly, she would have to fool both William and Don as well as the cast and crew of *Real People*.

The identical twins had often switched places as kids, especially when they were sent to boarding school. Their teachers could never tell them apart. They looked alike, dressed alike, sounded alike, and enjoyed playing tricks on their parents, friends, and teachers. When Danielle realized she couldn't shoot the next episode of the show and that her absence could possibly doom the series, she called Darcy for help, and Darcy readily agreed to come to her rescue. Connie agreed to give her the time off, and Mark graciously consented to her going back to New York, although he always hated being apart from his wife.

"This switching thing is getting to be a habit," he joked. "You two just did it in Washington over the Fourth."

"Yes." Darcy grinned. "And it never gets old. Thanks for going along with us again. It's really important to Danielle."

* * *

While Danielle was getting registered and settled in her hospital room, she explained, as methodically as she could, about how the show was filmed and what her part in the next episode involved. She described the cast of characters in detail. Darcy wasn't worried about the acting part. She was used to the television jargon and filming routines from her days on *Speaking of Sports with Donavan & Donavan*. But fooling William and Don would be the tricky part.

Darcy asked pointed questions about both men and their relationship with Danielle. Darcy had to know whether she should flirt with either or both of them, and she needed to understand the personal dynamics between her sister and these two vibrant but very different men. There was only so much Danielle could share with her sister while she was being poked, prodded, and examined by the hospital staff doctors and nurses. In the end, Darcy would have to depend on her own instincts.

"Don't worry about anything," Darcy reassured her sister. "We've switched places many times before, and I know I can pull this off. Just rest and get better. I'll call you if I have any questions. Keep your phone handy."

Danielle started to cry with gratitude. "Thank you, Darcy. I was so afraid my absence would mess up the show. I knew I could count on you."

"Always." She kissed her sister goodbye and left the hospital room on a mission to save Danielle's show.

When she was getting into an Uber to go back to the apartment, her phone rang. "Darcy?" a male voice asked.

"Yes, who's this?"

"It's Tony Gantz. Sorry it's taken me so long to get back to you, but your stepmother was hard to track down. The good news is, I've finally found her. The bad news is, she's shacked up with a guy ... that Brett Fletcher. I think he was the other witness against your husband. They're both on a heavy-duty booze bender. I don't think you'll get much information out of her unless you can sober her up."

"Oh God." Darcy felt excited but overwhelmed. "When it rains, it pours!"

CHAPTER 56

Darcy

Darcy arrived on the set early the next morning just like Danielle was accustomed to doing. She went into the makeup room and sat in Danielle's chair.

"Morning," Darcy said to Marcie, the makeup artist. "I got a lot of rest over the weekend, and my cough is almost gone. Hopefully I won't need much makeup today."

Marcie looked at her closely. "You do look much better. Terrific, in fact, Danielle. And I think you even put on a pound or two."

The two continued to chat while Marcie did her job. The hairdresser came in next and combed through Darcy's hair and sprayed it lightly. Then Darcy walked onto the set, which was an exact duplicate of the chemo suite at the hospital. She approached a handsome man standing off to the side with a clipboard in his hand.

"Good morning, Danielle." William greeted her warmly and kissed her on the cheek. "You look fabulous. You must be feeling better." He had been concerned because she seemed so tired and had a wicked cough.

"Yes. Thanks, William. I rested the whole weekend, and Lynn made me mashed potatoes and vanilla milkshakes to fatten me up. I'm still coughing a little, but now the Robitussin DM controls it. I honestly feel like my old self again."

Darcy found it easy to play the role of her sister and was having fun. This was just like old times. There was more at risk with this switch, but Darcy was up to the challenge.

"Do you want to run your lines before we start?" William asked, smiling at her. She was truly beautiful, and being near her made him feel on top of the world. And today she seemed to have a special glow. There was something a little different about her, but he couldn't tell what it was.

"No. I think I've got it. Where's Mary?" She was the actress hired to play one of the terminally ill cancer patients.

"Here I am," Mary called as she walked onto the set. "Good morning, Danielle, William. I'm ready to go."

Darcy and Mary took their places side by side. Mary reclined in the fake leather lounge chair, wearing a red bandanna secured around her head to hide her hair loss, and a bag of chemo drugs ostensibly dripped its poison into her vein. Darcy, dressed in a white lab coat, began reading Mary's journal. Soon other actresses and actors filled up all the chairs. The patients greeted each other and chatted among themselves until Darcy began the session by reading an excerpt from Mary's journal and then applying it to the lesson for the day.

The patients interacted with each other, supposedly spontaneously, but their words had been scripted to show off the program in a good light. Darcy continued leading the session and expertly urged each patient to read a part of their individual journals and then opened the session up to general discussion. She glanced often in William's direction for affirmation, and he gave her frequent thumbs-up signals, so she continued. William seemed satisfied with her performance. He certainly didn't appear to notice that the real Danielle had been replaced by her identical twin.

"Let's take a break for lunch," William announced after a few hours. "Everyone be back in an hour." He walked over to Darcy and draped his arm protectively over her shoulder. "Have a bite with me, Danielle. I want to run over this afternoon's script, and I have a suggestion about tomorrow's."

Darcy felt uneasy. She didn't want to put William off, and Danielle had warned her that William was attracted to her and often tried to hold her hand, rub against her, or grab her in tight hugs. This display made Danielle uncomfortable, but she put up with it, because she didn't want to jeopardize the show. Darcy wanted no part of being groped by William either and needed an excuse to refuse his lunch offer without offending him.

She noticed Don March was standing in the corner of the set with his arms folded tightly over his chest; he was glaring at William. He looked upset. She'd need to go to him and make sure he hadn't noticed anything suspicious. "I need to speak to Don," Darcy said a bit too quickly. "Can we talk a little later, please?"

William and Don exchanged menacing looks. Darcy couldn't help but grin at the sight of two grown men, who were obviously jealous of each other and behaving so childishly, vying for Danielle's affections. She thought they resembled two angry cowboys, gripping their gun holsters and anticipating an old-fashioned western movie shootout.

"No, it can't wait. I need to talk to you now," William insisted and pulled Darcy toward the makeshift cafeteria on the opposite side of the set. "We have to discuss a few things before we're ready for this afternoon."

Darcy felt helpless but knew she had to go along with him. She shot Don an apologetic look, shrugged, and followed William to the sandwich and beverage table.

"What's so damn important?" she asked a little too impatiently. "I don't like being dragged off like a naughty child."

William regarded her suspiciously. He had never known Danielle to be abrupt or rude. "What's wrong?" he asked in a soothing voice. "I just wanted to spend time with you and go over a few changes in the script." He constantly made up reasons to prolong their interactions. He couldn't get enough of Danielle, and since she refused to see him socially, he spent as much time as possible with her on the set or in professional meetings.

"Sorry." Darcy cast her eyes downward so William wouldn't see her annoyed expression. "I overreacted. I needed to talk to Don, but it can wait."

"No problem, my beauty." He pulled out the afternoon script and began discussing the lines he'd circled in red. "I don't think these words sound realistic. The dialogue is beginning to sound very stilted. We need it to sound more spontaneous—more natural—and not always speak in full sentences."

Oh Lord, what would Danielle say? Darcy thought. She had to react the way Danielle would. She personally agreed that the dialogue seemed fabricated, but would her sister?

"Excuse me, William. I need to powder my nose. I'll be right back." Darcy sprinted to the ladies' room before he could object. Once inside the toilet stall, she dialed Danielle and in a whispered voice explained the dialogue dilemma. After a brief conversation with her sister, Darcy returned to the set and approached the producer.

"I believe you're right about the dialogue," she said sweetly. "And if you recall, the original idea was to have real cancer patients speak in their own words, but then you went ahead and hired professional writers and actors. You said they would make the series appear more polished, but actually I think they make it look phony."

"I do remember saying that," William admitted sheepishly. "I guess I was wrong. But if you ever tell anyone that I admitted that, I'll categorically deny it." He grinned, and his deep-brown eyes twinkled. Darcy had to admit that the man was adorable. Why didn't Danielle think so? Or did she?

"Redoing some patient scenes will cost us another few weeks in production, but I believe the results will be worth it." Besides, he thought, *That will give me more time to win Danielle over.* "We should redo the patient segments … film them with real cancer victims, not actors."

"That's wonderful!" Darcy exclaimed exuberantly and spontaneously threw her arms around William. "That'll make such a difference." Then, realizing her mistake, she withdrew quickly and moved away from him. Danielle would never have done that. She would have been thrilled that they were going back to the original concept for the show, but she would have shown more physical restraint, especially since she was trying to subtly reject William's advances.

William was stunned but encouraged by Danielle's spontaneous outburst. She had never touched him before … and when he kissed her on her cheek this time, she hadn't flinched. She seemed warmer and more affectionate. The weekend of rest had produced a miraculous change in her. Maybe he'd been too quick to dismiss them as a possible couple. Could there be hope for the two of them? Time would tell.

Don had witnessed the whole exchange and was visibly upset. He was hurt by watching Danielle's interaction with William. She had repeatedly assured him that she wasn't romantically interested in the producer. Her actions told another story. It wasn't like Danielle to be so duplicitous. He stalked out of the room in disbelief and was enraged. But more than anything, he was disappointed and hurt.

Darcy, unaware of Don's hasty departure, returned to the set. She felt happy and proud, and was convinced that she had diverted a disaster. She was wrong.

CHAPTER 57

Danielle

Danielle lay in her hospital bed, anxious for Darcy to arrive.

"How did it go?" she asked her sister the minute Darcy entered the room. "Did anyone suspect you weren't me?"

"I don't think so," Darcy answered. "There were a few tense moments, however."

"Like what?" Danielle was dying to hear every detail. She loved the adventure of switching places with her sibling.

"Well, right around lunchtime, William had a sudden epiphany. He said the dialogue sounded phony, as I told you on the phone. I think he just wanted to spend more time with me—I mean, you. He admitted that he'd made a mistake by hiring actors and writers, and he agreed to redo some of the segments that should have been shot here at the hospital with real patients. I was so excited for you because I knew that's what you had wanted from the beginning. I spontaneously threw by arms around him and gave him a big hug."

Danielle looked at her askance. "OMG." Darcy was always full of mischief and was much more outgoing than she was. "That must have surprised him."

"I know, I know." Darcy was remorseful. "But he's very huggable, a really attractive man. It was a Darcy move, not a Danielle one. I think William was honestly so surprised that he didn't find my actions odd. Maybe he's a little more hopeful now that something may develop between you two, but tomorrow I'll put a stop to that notion. I promise. I'm sorry if I've made things difficult for you."

"Wait a minute." Danielle grinned. "Sit down here on the bed, and let's think about this. William has definitely shown an interest in me, but I don't pretend to think I'm the only woman on his radar screen. He's a player and always flirting with someone. He seems to collect women like I collect scarves. It might be fun for you to string him along and teach him a lesson. I bet not many women turn him down."

"Seriously? That would be so much fun, but wouldn't that put your series in jeopardy?" Darcy didn't want to make matters worse for Danielle, and she knew how much promoting Healing Words and Healing Hands meant to her sister.

"I don't think so," Danielle said soberly. "How on earth could William know about our switching places unless we tell him? And once we do, when the truth becomes public, it will probably increase the show's ratings by a lot. Viewers will be curious and want to tune in."

Darcy was quiet for a moment, absorbing what her sister proposed. "How far do you want to take this?"

"I'm not sure. I don't want to be mean to William. He's really a nice man, but I wouldn't mind putting him in his place, just a little … not only for me but for all the women he's probably tried to seduce."

"That's a lofty justification for having a little fun with the man." Darcy giggled. "But, okay, I'll be my flirtatious best. As long as I have to play you for another few days, I might as well have some fun. But I'll only go so far—remember, I'm a happily married woman."

A hospital volunteer brought in Danielle's dinner tray. Darcy stayed another few minutes longer, discussing their plan, and then went home to play with her niece and nephew, learn her lines for the next day, and call the private investigator, Tony Gantz, back.

CHAPTER 58

Darcy

Darcy again arrived bright and early on the set. Today's session called for her to lead a round-table discussion about Healing Hands with prominent physicians from the hospital staff, and then she would introduce Don March. Darcy realized how important this segment was to Danielle, and she wanted it to go perfectly. Many of the participants were friends of Danielle and Alex, so she had to be very careful to act exactly as Danielle would. The plan to flirt with William would have to wait until after the taping was complete.

"Good morning, my beauty." William approached her and gave her an intimate hug. Darcy tried not to flinch and forced herself not to pull away.

"Hello," Darcy replied casually, pretending to be distracted. She didn't want to give William a chance to turn the conversation into a personal one. "How long is this segment? I want to be sure to leave enough time to properly introduce Don and give him enough time to talk."

"We've allotted twenty minutes for the panel discussion and then two minutes for you to introduce Dr. March. Then he has fifteen minutes to talk about Healing Words and launch Healing Hands."

"That's perfect." Darcy smiled and quickly moved to take her position in the circle of chairs laid out for the scene. She was surprised when William sat down next to her and put his arm possessively along the back of her seat.

"We have a few minutes before we need to get started," he whispered. "I've been thinking about us."

She was tempted to say, "There *is* no us," but kept silent and allowed him to continue.

"You're an exciting and sexy woman, Danielle. You need a man in your life, even if you don't think you're ready for one. I think I can be that man. It's time to stop mourning your husband and grab the brass ring. You should know that life is very short ... and it's for the living."

She gave him a playful look but made no comment. There was a thin line between encouragement and rejection. She didn't want to ruin anything for her sister.

William looked at her in earnest. He admired Danielle. She was smart and provocative yet honest, and she didn't play the silly games other woman did. He liked that about her. He was a game player himself but saw how shallow it could be at times. Up until now, he had always needed a variety of women to keep him satisfied, but there was something special about his feelings for Danielle. He wasn't sure, but he wondered if he could give up his old ways and become a one-woman man for her. He knew she would tolerate nothing less. He'd have to think about it more. These feelings for Danielle were so unusual for him.

"How about dinner tonight? There's a new French restaurant that just opened in the village?"

Darcy was about to refuse when William leaned closer, subtlety nibbled her ear, and whispered, "It's been a long time since Alex passed. You can't remain celibate forever."

Darcy recoiled as she knew Danielle would have. She was offended. How dare William invoke dear Alex's name as part of his seduction. She had been thinking she and Danielle had misread him? But now she realized leopards never change their spots. Once a player, always a player.

Darcy didn't have time to reject William's unwelcome dinner invitation or vent her anger toward him for invoking Alex's name, because Don marched into the circle of chairs and angrily took a seat directly opposite her. His nostrils flared, and his eyes shot daggers.

Darcy suddenly grasped what the expression "if looks could kill" meant. She wondered if his distain was meant for her or for William. He was clearly angry and looked on the verge of throwing a temper tantrum.

William, seemingly oblivious to the tension in the room, stood up to begin the session. "Lights, cameras, action," he called out from habit. "Let's begin."

Darcy did her best to engage the other doctors in a meaningful dialogue. She kept looking at Don for support and reassurance, but he remained incensed and was doing a slow burn. His eyes drilled into her so intensely that she had to turn away.

William called for a five-minute break and approached Danielle. "Have a cup of coffee with me," he suggested in a sultry voice and led her to the beverage table, casually placing his hand on her butt. "And then you can introduce Dr. March for his segment."

Darcy made an excuse and fled to the ladies' room. This time when she called Danielle, she was beyond furious. "The man is insufferable," she wailed. "I don't think I can continue this charade. He's coming on way too strong and disrespecting Alex."

Danielle was alarmed. Darcy almost never lost her cool. "Try to stay calm," she begged. "The doctors are sending me home tomorrow, so you'll only have to do this for one more day. Please, Darcy. This show is so important to me and to my tribute for Alex. Please stay the course for a little while longer."

Darcy relented. "I know, I know. Okay, one more day but only because I love you. And you owe me big time, little sister. After this filming is done, I don't think either one of us should have anything to do with William Bell. He's not a harmless flirt. He's a cocky womanizer."

"Agreed," Danielle said thankfully. She needed Darcy to finish taping the segment. It was the climax of the entire series when Don as executive director of Healing Word and Healing Hands would discuss the financial aspects of the program and try to solicit donations and support from the public.

"You know, I'm not trying to justify William's behavior at all, but when I first met Don March, I thought he was a loud-mouthed, self-centered oaf. My first impression was dead wrong. He's a great guy and my best friend (sister excepted). I don't know how I could have survived Alex's death or moved the programs forward without him. Maybe we need to cut William a little slack. After all, men will be men." She laughed, trying to lighten the tension.

"I think you mean 'boys will be boys.' But your point?" Darcy asked sarcastically. She couldn't help but think back to the irresponsible reporter who had started bogus rumors about Nathan and her in the White House. "Boys will be boys" didn't cut it for her. Men had to be held responsible for their behavior. There were consequences for bad behavior.

"I'm just saying, don't be so quick to judge William. After all, he did see the value in my programs and is responsible for creating the television show."

"Whatever," Darcy replied. Danielle was naive. Darcy knew a playboy when she saw one, no matter how charming and delightful he seemed. "Let me get back in there and get this show over with. I'll see you later."

Darcy resumed her place back in the circle. She stifled her anger toward William and began her gracious introduction of Dr. Don March, explaining his credentials and his value and contributions to the program.

"I am so pleased to present Dr. Don March, our executive director, and to hear what he has to say." Darcy turned to Don and smiled warmly.

Don took the microphone from Danielle. He stood erect and faced the cameras. With one sharp glare at the producer and then back at Danielle, he said, "I quit."

CHAPTER 59

Danielle

Danielle was happy to be at home and surrounded by her children. She felt much better. The antibiotics were working, and her cough was greatly diminished. Her color was good, and her appetite had returned. She felt ready to go back to work, although her doctors advised that she rest for a few more days.

Danielle planned to defy them. It was time for her to finish the filming project with William and get back to her work with Don at Healing Words. She missed their conversations and the day-to-day running of the program with him. They made a good team and worked well together. Filming had been fun but was only a small part of what Healing Words was all about. Danielle needed to return to the office and spend more time with Don, the staff, and especially the patients.

Lynn had prepared a lasagna supper for Danielle, the children, and Darcy. The dining room table was set, and only the salad needed tossing. Danielle decanted a bottle of cabernet to thank her sister for coming to New York and switching places with her to hide Danielle's health issues and save the show. Darcy had been gracious and selfless, but it was time for her to go home to her life in Washington with Mark and the Pierces.

Darcy stormed breathlessly into the apartment and scooped up Caroline and Freddy for giant hugs. The children were so adorable. They had a calming effect on her. "Can we hold off on dinner for a while?" she asked, noticing the table was set in the dining room with Danielle's good china and silverware. "I need to talk to you first."

"Sure, it's early, and the wine's in the decanter. Pour us each a glass please, and I'll settle the kids in with a movie while we talk."

Darcy impatiently paced around the room, waiting for Danielle to return.

"You won't believe what happened today," she blurted as soon as Danielle reappeared.

"What? William again?" Danielle looked at her sister suspiciously. This was the second time in as many days that Darcy had been upset by something happening on the set. Maybe switching places hadn't been a good idea after all.

"No." Darcy gulped her wine. "It wasn't William. It was Don. He quit."

"He what?" Danielle wasn't sure she had heard accurately.

"When I introduced him, as we had planned, he grabbed the microphone and simply blurted out, 'I quit.' Then he stalked off the set. I tried running after him, but he refused to look at me or say another word."

"That doesn't sound like Don at all. Let me call him right now and get to the bottom of this. There has to be a reasonable explanation." Danielle was mortified. She couldn't imagine Healing Words without Don, her best friend. She dialed his phone, but it went straight to voice mail. Danielle knew he had caller ID and would immediately see that it was her. He would never ignore her unless something was terribly wrong. She redialed his number and left a message.

"Don, it's Danielle. Damn it, I have no idea what's going on with you, but we have to settle whatever this is *tonight*! I will not go to bed until you come over here and explain why you quit. I'll be waiting here for as long as it takes."

"That ought to get his attention," Darcy said dryly. "What's with the men in your life nowadays? They're all lunatics."

"So it would seem," Danielle answered. She was more upset than she cared to admit and devastated that Don may have been serious about resigning. She hadn't realized how much she cared about him and counted on him every day.

"I'm not hungry anymore," Danielle said forlornly. "Let's feed the kids so I can put them to bed before Don gets here. I have to straighten this out."

CHAPTER 60

Danielle, Darcy, and Don

Darcy opened the door when the bell rang. Danielle was in the children's bedroom, reading them a bedtime story.

"I don't like being ordered around," Don said without preamble when he walked angrily through the door. Out of habit he patted Hippocrates on his head and turned to confront Danielle. "This is ridiculous. You know perfectly well why I'm so ticked off. I don't like being made a fool of, especially in public. I never expected this from you."

Danielle walked into the living room, still carrying the children's bedtime storybook in her hand. She hadn't heard the doorbell but immediately saw Don's angry face. She couldn't help but smile. No matter how annoyed she was with him, it was funny to see him do a double take and gaze back and forth between Darcy and her. She had always loved the stunned reaction people had when they saw the two twins standing side by side.

He looked at the woman he thought was Danielle. "Darcy, right?" He remembered her from the awful days surrounding Alex's death. "Frankly I can't tell you apart."

"Yes, that's right, but I'm Danielle." She chuckled as she approached Don. "If you'd been able to tell us apart, we couldn't have pulled off the switch that fooled William Bell and the entire cast and crew of *Real People*. Now what's this garbage I hear about you quitting?"

Don scrutinized both women, but other than their clothes, they were totally alike. He didn't know which one to talk to. "I thought we had a special friendship, actually more than a friendship." He began nervously speaking to first one sister and then the other. "But your behavior with William in the last two days has killed me. I can't take it anymore. I feel like such an idiot thinking we had something special between us, only to see you shamelessly flirting with another man for all the world and our professional colleagues to see. The last two days have been humiliating, to say the least. Under the circumstances, I can't be around you anymore. It hurts too much." He sat down dejectedly. He had poured his heart out to Danielle and in front of her sister. He felt like a fool.

"I'm so sorry, Don," the real Danielle admitted shamefully. "Sit down and let me explain what's been going on. But suffice it to say, it was Darcy you were seeing the last few days on the set. She was covering for me. We switched places to hide the fact that I've been in the hospital with pneumonia. I didn't want William to know. I was afraid he'd cancel the show."

"That's true," Darcy piped up. "I'm sorry if our switching places hurt you, Don. I never thought about that aspect of our plan. I was just having fun leading William on … giving him some of his own medicine and helping keep Danielle's secret. I guess it backfired."

"We just wanted to keep the filming on track and not give William an excuse to cancel or delay the project," Danielle confessed. "I was afraid that if he thought I might be absent for a while, he'd lose interest in the program and turn his attentions elsewhere. He's very flighty. I'm sorry that Darcy and I didn't think our idea through more carefully, and we should have told you the truth."

Don was still astonished by the twin's look-alike appearance and the fact that on the set he hadn't even suspected that Danielle wasn't who she appeared to be. If he had been fooled, obviously so had the producer and the entire television crew.

"I guess I have to apologize for my churlish behavior," he said meekly. "I should have had more faith in you. I'm sorry for jumping to the wrong conclusions. May I retract my stupid resignation? Please, Danielle. I'm so sorry. It seems that I've had to apologize for my boorish behavior more than once."

"Of course." She laughed in relief. "I'm so glad this farce is finally over, but we'll still have to film the finale again since you so ungraciously quit on the last take."

"Yes, I did." He groaned. "But I'll smooth things over with William. Then we can wrap up that last segment and get back to our real work ... and our real relationship," he said hopefully.

Danielle smiled warmly at Don. "We'll have plenty of time to figure out what's going on between us. Let's just wrap this taping thing up first."

Don nodded and hugged Danielle gratefully. He was so relieved that she wasn't interested in William. Then he suddenly realized what she had said. "OMG. You were in the hospital. For how long? Are you all right now?"

Darcy and Danielle burst out laughing. They knew everything was going to be all right.

CHAPTER 61

Darcy

Darcy took the train to DC. She was anxious to get back to Mark. As the train pulled out of the station in Wilmington, Delaware, she dialed the private investigator's cell phone number. "Hello, Tony. It's Darcy Donavan. Sorry it's taken so long for me to get back to you. I've been in New York on family business. Tell me that you found my rotten stepmother."

"Hi, Darcy," he replied, happy to hear from her. He had interesting news to share. "I've tracked Karin down, as I told you in my last message. She's living in a flophouse on the Bowery with a man named Brett Fletcher. They are both unemployed and heavily into the booze scene."

"She's in New York?" Darcy was surprised. She had thought Karin moved miles away from the city after everything that had happened.

"Yes, she's back," he explained. "After the debacle over your father's will, she moved to Atlanta, where she worked as a high-priced escort in Buckhead. That didn't pan out, so she moved and took a job as a cocktail waitress at the Perch Bar in Baltimore. That job lasted only a few months until she was fired for stealing from the tips jar. The owner of the establishment agreed not to file charges as long as she left the city within twenty-four hours. Apparently, he was 'hot' for her and didn't want to see her go to prison. She eventually ended up back in New York, and she and Brett reconnected and have been pulling scams all around the city to earn enough cash to keep them in vodka. They've been arrested twice, but the police couldn't make the charges stick."

"Well, maybe we can make the ESPN charges stick and bring her down once and for all. You have her address, I assume?"

"Yes, I'll text it your phone. Is there anything else I can do for you?"

"I don't think so, Tony, but thanks for your hard work. You have my address, so if you've used up your retainer, send me a bill for the balance."

"Will do." Tony was about to hang up when Darcy had an afterthought.

"Did you find out anything about Karin's companion, that guy, Brett Fletcher? I'm sure he's the same man she was involved with years ago when she cheated on my father, and the two of them stole his fortune."

"That would be the same scumbag. He's had a colorful past. He went from being a mucky-muck CEO of his own investment company to slinging hash at the New York Deli on Broadway. Then he took a series of odd jobs and had several minor brushes with the law. So far, he's been able to avoid imprisonment. The two of them make quite a pair. I can't believe you're related to her."

"I'm *not!*" Darcy answered indignantly. "She's no blood relation … only a scheming, greedy whore who drew my vulnerable, unsuspecting father into her vicious web and then made everyone in our family miserable."

"Tell me how you really feel about her." Tony laughed loudly. "Wow!"

Darcy ignored his remark. Nothing made her more upset than thinking about Karin and what she'd done to the family. "She must have stewed for years after being shut out of Father's will and wanted revenge. She was obviously hell bent on punishing us, and I suppose getting Mark fired was certainly a good way. I don't know exactly how she pulled it off, but I need to tell my husband, and then we'll pay the conniving couple a little visit."

CHAPTER 62

Danielle

Danielle was thankful all the taping sessions were over and she was done with her part of the film project. When they taped Don's segment again, she had been polite but cool to William. He seemed confused but thankfully didn't make any more moves on her. He seemed to sense that Don and she had a new understanding, and to his credit, he backed away. She saw no reason to tell him about the switch. It would serve no purpose and might embarrass him. William thanked Danielle for her hard work and promised to host a preview party when the shows aired. She readily accepted his invitation. It would be fun to watch the show on the television instead of from the set.

Danielle and Don settled into a comfortable routine of meeting every morning for coffee at the office or in her apartment if she was working from home. They discussed the plans for the day and bounced new ideas off each other. The network's announcement that a television show had been made about the Healing Words and Healing Hands programs generated a lot of interest in the community, and the number of new patients signed up from all around the city.

"Alex would be very proud," Danielle said wistfully. "I can't believe he's been gone over a year, and yet it feels like just yesterday that Caroline was born and had to start off her young life without a father." Her voice cracked, but she didn't cry.

"You're doing a wonderful job raising that precious little lady, and Freddy gets cuter and cuter each day." Don took Danielle's hand. "You should be very proud of yourself as a mother. I know Alex would be."

Danielle had stopped seeing her psychiatrist, Dr. Dorien. Now, when she felt the need to vent, she called her friend Ray Smith in Boston, or Darcy or in most cases spoke directly with Don.

Holidays and anniversaries came and went. Danielle struggled and survived them all with courage. She had endured the unimaginable pain and loneliness of sudden grief. While still missing Alex every day, she had learned coping techniques and had become quite independent and strong. She was no longer afraid of facing the future without a husband by her side. She still had some bad days; however, they were fewer and fewer and farther and farther apart.

She was thankful she had Don to rely on. He was always available, and she often talked with him about his own personal losses. His wife, Rachelle, and his infant daughter, Carly, were always in his heart, but his heart was big enough for another love. He tried daily to convince Danielle that hers was big enough too. She thought he might be right, but she couldn't take off her wedding ring or commit to another man yet.

Danielle had always enjoyed writing and had published a modestly successful novel years ago. After that she had turned her writing talents into lesson guides and vignettes for her Healing Words program. Now she felt a constant tugging on her soul to write another novel. She had lived through the horrific experience of losing a spouse and wanted that pain and her newfound understanding to be the centerpiece of her next endeavor.

At night after the children were in bed, she sat at her computer and pounded away for hours, caught up in her story and completely losing track of time. In the morning, she shared what she had written with Don, and they collaborated. He shared the intimate moments of his own grief, and she wove his emotions and revelations into the plot. At times she thought the book was almost more about his journey through grief than about her own, but she didn't mind. The story was poignant and cathartic to write. She didn't want to share it with anyone else, not even Darcy, until it was completely finished. She felt like she was pregnant and about to give birth to it. The completed manuscript would be like her delivering a baby book, complete with its chapters and characters, like little fingers and toes. She knew it was a corny analogy but nonetheless true. And she was very protective of it, just like with Freddy and Caroline.

She finished the book in July when Caroline was a year and a half years old and little Freddy was almost four. She celebrated by renting a beach house for ten days in August in the seaside town of Ocean City, Maryland. Darcy and Mark joined her and the children. They all had a wonderful vacation, filled with sunshine, sand, saltwater taffy, miniature golf, and ice cream cones from a shop on the boardwalk.

Danielle had wanted to invite Don to come with them, but they hadn't been physically intimate yet, and she felt having him there might give the wrong impression to the children. She talked to him several times a day, however, and told him how much she missed him. As much as she wanted to be with Don, she was determined not to do anything that would upset her children.

They were used to Don by now. They called him "Doc D." He was always around their house, playing games with them, sharing meals, and watching movies, but Danielle had been careful not to make it appear that he was replacing their dad. She kept Alex's memories alive by showing the kids pictures of their father and telling them stories about him. Freddy barely remembered him, and Caroline had never known him. Until she and Don decided what their relationship was and where it was going, he would remain Doc D to her children.

Before leaving for the beach, Danielle had sent sample pages of her manuscript with query letters to several prominent literary agents and was anxiously awaiting their replies. In the meantime, because of the experience of writing the book, she'd come up with another idea of an additional program to compliment Healing Words and Healing Hands. She was excited about coming back to the city and sharing the concept with Don.

Darcy and Mark were returning with her to spend another week in New York. Connie and Nathan were away at their Massachusetts summer home on the Cape, and Congress was in recess. It was a perfect time for Darcy and Mark to take time off from their White House duties. Darcy had hinted to Danielle that she had mysterious business to handle in the city and that it involved Karin.

CHAPTER 63

Darcy and Mark were glad to be back in their New York condo. They had missed the vibrance of the city. They loved taking long walks through the city streets or taking Danielle's children to the park and the zoo. They were anonymous in the city. In Washington someone always recognized one or the other of them and boldly interrupted them to chat or seek an autograph. Mark never lost his patience and always posed for pictures or selfies. While the politics and excitement of the White House were contagious, nothing compared to an egg cream from Katz's deli or a hot dog from Nathan's.

After a few days of enjoying the city, Mark and Darcy became serious about their mission to implicate Karin in Mark's firing debacle. They visited Bill Robinson and discussed their options. What could they do to legally trap Karin into making a confession? And if she confessed and they recorded it, would the tape be admissible in the court of law? They wanted Karin to be held accountable and weren't opposed to jail time as her punishment.

Bill Robinson carefully explained the New York laws of admissible evidence to them. "New York," he said, "is a one-party consent state. That means that if Darcy is talking to Karin alone, the recording of that conversation can be used as evidence because Darcy knows she was being taped. If, however, without their knowledge Darcy records Brett and Karin speaking to each other, that conversation wouldn't be admissible.

The exception is if the conversation takes place in a public place; then there is a reasonable assumption that other people in the area could overhear it. That recording would be legal."

"Do you see the difference?" he asked Darcy and Mark. "It's a clear distinction. If you go to the effort of getting her to confess, you don't want the evidence thrown out of court."

"Yes," Mark answered. "I understand. The safest thing to do is for Darcy or me to try to get Karin alone. The other option is to lure Brett and Karin to a public place and make sure other people are nearby and can overhear us talking."

"Yes, that's it, exactly. Let me know how it goes." The lawyer walked Darcy and Mark back to the elevator bank in his office. "You have the element of surprise on your side. Karin will not be expecting to run into you. She thinks you're living in DC, so hopefully you can get her to admit she planned the whole thing and then took money to stay quiet. Remember, she's not the brightest bulb in the chandelier, as you know from past experience. Brett's a different story. He's cunning and ruthless. Remember how he forged Fred Coulter's signature on those stock certificates and then transferred the stocks into his own private account? Your best bet is to get Karin alone."

"I will make it happen," Darcy said with steely determination. "And by the end of this week."

"You go, girl." Mark laughed. "Nothing like a woman scorned. I can't wait to see this play out."

"It's not about me," Darcy protested. "She had you fired and our show canceled by validating false charges and committing perjury. She needs her day of reckoning."

CHAPTER 64

Danielle

Danielle was happy that Darcy and Mark had extended their New York visit through the upcoming weekend. Her sister was being mysterious about their reason for staying the few extra days but promised to tell Danielle everything soon. Darcy asked Danielle to plan a family dinner and insisted that Don be included. She saw him as an important part of Danielle's life, even if Danielle wasn't willing to admit it yet. Danielle smiled coquettishly and agreed.

Danielle decided that since it was to be a celebration of some sort, she would forgo her normal casserole entree and make roast beef, complete with mint peas, roasted potatoes, and a Caesar salad. Don volunteered to help. He was a good cook, and they enjoyed being in the kitchen together. They had spent most of the day preparing the meal … setting the table with the good china and silverware inherited from Danielle's father, marinating the roast, and making a lemon meringue pie.

As they worked side by side, everything about the experience felt comfortable and natural. Danielle glanced over at Don, who was busy peeling the potatoes and playing a game with Freddy at the same time. Apparently, she wasn't the only one who could multitask. She wondered whether she was being silly in refusing to consider a more permanent relationship with him.

Don was a kind, loving, decent man, who clearly adored her and her children. He had waited patiently for her to signal that she wanted more from him than simply being her business partner or a sounding board. What was holding her back? Was she afraid of another loss? She studied him again. He was so affectionate with Freddy and always doing whatever she asked of him. He had become, like the Elton John song said, "the winds beneath my wings." Shouldn't being with a loving, caring person be enough for her? More and more she thought about Don and what a future with him could look like.

"I had an idea," she said, trying to refocus her thoughts.

"About what?" he asked.

"Don't think me crazy, but when I was working on my book, I realized that by the very act of writing it, I was stepping through my grief and gaining insight. Talking to you about Rachelle and Carly helped so much too. I became aware that the idea of expressive writing could be applied to everyone dealing with their own personal tragedies, whether it be the loss of a spouse or a child, even a close friend."

"And?" Don suspected he knew where Danielle was going with this new revelation but he wanted to hear it from her.

"And," she continued boldly, "what if we extended our Helping Words and Helping Hands programs to encompass compassionate grief counseling? We could call it Helping Hearts." Danielle held her breath, waiting for his reaction. She wouldn't move forward with this new idea unless he agreed that it had potential. She needed his positive reinforcement and support.

Don put down the potato peeler and smiled affectionately at her. "That's a fabulous idea. There are grief support programs like Compassionate Friends that have been around for over forty years. But to my knowledge, none incorporate the expressive writing concept. Do you see it as a separate entity under our existing umbrella or as a new endeavor altogether?"

"I don't really know," she said thoughtfully. "I haven't matured the idea completely. I wanted to get your reaction first. Maybe it should be a new one that embraces all the others … coping with serious illnesses, mentoring medical students and young physicians, and compassionate grieving counseling. Then, if we find additional needs, we can always add more and more programs. For lack of a better description, we'd be kind of like the United Way of expressive writing therapies."

He laughed. "Well said. Let's feed the kids lunch and put them down for their naps. Then you and I can spend the afternoon working on this new idea. I think you really have a great concept, but at first glance, it needs a little refining. You can afford to take on the additional financial cost from the monies from your inheritance, but I don't believe you should. We need to explore the idea of finding outside investors and probably starting a foundation."

"Sounds good to me." Danielle was thrilled by Don's positive response, happy that he had accepted her idea so readily and was offering to help. She thought about their future again. The comfort and security of knowing Don was always there, supporting and encouraging her, loving her and her children, could be enough … more than enough. Maybe the man she should spend the rest of her life with was right there, standing in her kitchen with a potato peeler in one hand and holding her daughter with the other.

Spontaneously she walked over to him and gently moved his face to within inches of hers. She looked into his eyes and placed her lips on his. She was surprised by the intense feelings that single kiss engendered.

Don gently put Caroline down and swooped Danielle into his arms. He returned her kiss ardently and pressed her body against his, moaning in delight. "Darling Danielle, I've waited forever for this moment." He kissed her again more deeply and then again and again.

CHAPTER 65

Darcy

Darcy and Mark stood outside the flophouse hotel on the lower east side, observing the comings and goings of the motley patrons. Bowery bums, winos, and homeless people streamed in and out of the decrepit door.

"This is truly how I pictured skid row," Darcy said with disdain. "How can people live like this?"

"It's certainly not by choice. It's probably their only option. Most of these poor creatures are homeless, jobless, and living only for the next drink or drug."

"I'm not unsympathetic about people who have had genuine hardships in their lives and are forced to live in awful places like this, but look at them. Most are able-bodied, middle-aged men and women, who could get a decent job if they were so inclined. Instead they're living off the rest of us and spending their welfare checks on booze." She rolled her eyes in disgust but kept focused on the front door. She was waiting for Karin to emerge … and hopefully alone.

They didn't have long to wait. Karin Coulter came out of the hotel by herself and started walking hastily up the street. It was cold, and she hugged her thin sweater coat to her body for warmth. Darcy was shocked by her stepmother's slovenly appearance. The woman she remembered had practically lived in the neighborhood beauty shop. She had always had immaculately coiffed and professionally colored hair and beautifully manicured nails polished in the brightest shade of red. Her makeup had always been expertly applied, and she wore long, mink eyelashes. She had walked around like a haughty fashion model, strutting down the runway, dressed in designer clothes, and dripping with jewelry. But not now.

Today she wore a long, ugly, brown tweed skirt that hung well below her knees and seemed several sizes too big for her slim figure, a stained white blouse, and an ugly gray sweater coat with several missing buttons. Her once-white athletic shoes were badly soiled, and the left sole was ripping off. She clutched a plastic purse that matched the color of her cheap-looking pink lipstick. She could easily have stolen her outfit from any trash can on the Bowery or from a sleezy thrift shop. But her nails were immaculate and polished in her signature red color. She must have forgone a drink or two in favor of a weekly manicure.

Mark was as disturbed by the sight of Karin's disheveled appearance as Darcy had been. "My God," he said with surprise. "How the mighty have fallen. She looks like a character from a Charles Dickens novel. Let's follow her so you can try to catch her alone. Do you have you phone set to record?"

"Yes, it's in my pocket. Is yours on too, in case we need a backup?"

He nodded and patted his overcoat pocket. They started down the street after Karin, keeping far enough back so she wouldn't sense she was being followed. After three blocks, Karin entered a dilapidated liquor store and disappeared inside. Darcy and Mark walked into the same shop a few seconds later.

"Showtime," Mark remarked sarcastically. "It's time for stepmother dearest to have a little family reunion ... somewhere between the bourbon and the vodka bottles."

CHAPTER 66

Danielle

Danielle was mortified that she'd been so bold and spontaneously kissed Don. She had never behaved that impulsively before and was embarrassed by her aggressiveness. Don didn't appear to mind. As a matter of fact, he quickly helped her put together the children's lunches and practically shoved the sandwiches down their throats. He wanted to put them to bed for their naps and have Danielle all to himself.

When he finally had her alone, he took her in his arms and kissed her repeatedly. "Whoa, wait a minute." She giggled breathlessly. "This is all happening too fast."

"Not fast enough in my opinion." He winked and kissed her deeply again. This time he nibbled her lower lips and blew his warm breath into her ear. The taste of her lips was delicious. He was intoxicated by the smell of her floral perfume. When she protested, he reluctantly let her go, and they went to sit at the kitchen table to talk. The dining room was already set for their dinner later that night with Mark and Darcy.

"Let's go over more specifics about your grief idea," he said quietly, trying to regain his composure. "I'm excited about it."

"Excited about it or about something else." She laughed, noticing his erection.

"That too." He grinned and slid his knees farther under the table.

"I've been thinking." She tried to return the conversation to her new idea. "This new program should be about healing and surviving. We successfully help cancer patients learn to live with their diagnosis and the consequences, then we should be able to teach the bereaved special survival techniques for their situation and coping mechanisms too … and do it all through expressive writing exercises that I'll write to guide them."

"Then going forward, it would seem we're talking about a three-pronged program under one general umbrella. I think we should form a foundation to fund it and change the name to embrace all three programs: Healing Words, Healing Hands, and Healing Hearts. That's too much of a mouthful."

"Do you have a new name in mind?" she asked. "I agree there are too many words. Can you imagine the letterhead? It would take up the whole page."

"Not yet, but we can proceed without a specific one for the moment. We need to pick a board of directors, get our attorneys working on the legal aspects. and plan some fundraising events. I'm sure the right name will come to us along the way."

"It sounds like a massive undertaking." She was almost overwhelmed by the scope of it. "I'm willing to do it but only if you'll be by my side and consider being the co-CEO and running the whole program with me." She couldn't imagine doing this without him. It was a daunting and worthwhile endeavor but would require too much of her time and energy while raising two small children.

"Let me think about that." He smiled warmly. "If I took the position, it would mean that I'd have to spend almost every waking hour with you, I suppose, and maybe nights too. That's a pretty big commitment. I guess if you twisted my arm, I could be persuaded to say yes."

"What exactly would it take to persuade you?" She looked at him provocatively.

"Another kiss would be a good start." He grinned. "And the key to this apartment."

"What?" She was startled. She hadn't expected this. "Why do you need a key?" *Was he suggesting moving in with her?* She wasn't sure she was ready for that. They had only kissed a few times and hadn't made love, though the idea was intriguing. This was a pivotal moment in her life, and she knew it.

"Because if we're going to live together, my darling Danielle," he explained patiently, noting her confusion, "I don't want to keep ringing the doorbell and asking the nanny to let me into my own home."

He had willingly opened his heart to her and risked everything. Now he held his breath, waiting for her answer.

CHAPTER 67

Darcy

Darcy sneaked silently down the aisle where the gin and vodka bottles were on display. Karin was standing in the middle of them. Mark moved quietly down the adjacent one, where the scotch and bourbon liters lined the shelves.

Darcy maneuvered herself right up behind Karin, who was studying the bottles of vodka. Darcy tapped her stepmother solidly on the shoulder. Karin jerked around in surprise, afraid it was the cops trying to nail her for shoplifting again. She quickly put the bottle she'd been about to steal back on the shelf.

"I didn't do anything," she barked defensively before she noticed who was standing there. "Darcy, Danielle?" After all these years she still didn't know which girl was which.

"It's me, Darcy. Imagine my running into you here?" she said sarcastically. "Strange coincidence."

Darcy had thought maybe when she was face-to-face with Karin again, she would feel some tiny semblance of sympathy for her stepmother, but her revulsion was as strong as ever. Not only did she despise Karin for the despicable things she'd done, but she blamed her for getting Mark fired. She didn't have any concrete proof but was determined to bluff her way through the confrontation with the information the private investigator had given her. Hopefully she could make Karin feel trapped and force her to tell the truth.

"Why are you here?" Karin asked suspiciously, beginning to shake. She needed a shot of vodka to calm her nerves. It had been a few hours since she'd had a drink. "I thought you lived in DC and hung out with the president these days."

"I do, but I came to New York specifically to find you. There are a few things we need to straighten out."

"Oh?" Karin felt perspiration trickle down between her silicon-enhanced breasts. "Kindly leave me alone. We said all we had to say to each other years ago."

Darcy stood her ground. "That was before your latest act of revenge. I've come to warn you that I have definite proof that you lied under oath and arranged to have my husband fired on trumped-up charges. That's a federal crime, stepmother dearest, and you're going to pay for it. If you think living in a flophouse is rough, wait until you try prison life."

"I have no idea what you're talking about." Karin glared at Darcy, twisting her purse in her hand nervously. "You were always a self-centered brat. Get out of my way." She tried to shove Darcy, but Darcy remained firmly in place, blocking Karin's exit.

"Karin, I'm telling you, this can go down one of two ways. Either you confess to me right now, or you can take your chances before a judge and jury."

"You're bluffing." Karin snorted. Her shakes were getting worse, and she needed a drink badly. "You don't know a damn thing. Leave me alone and go back to the fucking White House."

Darcy didn't flinch. "Do you remember a man named Sonny Kasem? He had the hots for you and owned the Perch Bar in Baltimore where you worked, or should I say whored?"

Karin froze. Her eyes grew huge, and she inadvertently peed her pants. Darcy's accusations were right on target. Karin was terrified. She didn't want to go to jail and had to get away.

"Well, do you remember him, Karin?" Darcy persisted. "I'll jog your memory. You worked at his bar as a cocktail waitress, and off hours, he was your pimp. You had him wrapped around your little finger, just like you did my poor father." Darcy glared at the evil woman. "Have you no shame?"

Karin remained rigid, afraid of what was coming next. She was barely breathing. She knew she was trapped. There was no way out of the aisle without physically knocking Darcy to the floor.

"There was never enough money to make you happy," Darcy continued, "so you helped yourself to some of Sonny's bar receipts. Does any of this sound familiar? Don't pretend you don't know what I'm talking about."

Karin's head felt like it would explode, and she was uncomfortable standing around in her soiled, damp underwear. *How did Darcy find out about Baltimore? Did Sonny rat me out?*

Darcy thought for sure that when she mentioned Sonny's name, Karin would cave, but she hadn't yet. Darcy reached into her purse and pulled out a picture of the bar owner Tony Gantz had given her. She shoved the photo in Karin's face. "One more chance, or I'll take everything I know to the cops."

"Oh God." Karin crumpled to the ground, defeated, and began wailing. She couldn't keep up the innocent act any longer. She was beginning serious alcohol withdrawal. She shook all over and was going to puke.

"What do you want?" she hissed. "Haven't you and your damn family taken enough from me?"

"I think you have that backward. It's you who forged my father's signature and stole all his stocks." Darcy was furious. Karen had no conscience or remorse. "You ruined our family, and now you've tried to destroy my husband's career. You are an evil, evil woman."

Darcy decided to change tactics. She spoke more gently this time. "I want you to tell me the truth … and if you do, I'll make you a deal. I'll buy you that booze you were about to steal. Either that or Mark and I will go to the police and let them handle you. There's no vodka in interrogation rooms and certainly none in jail."

"Mark? He's here too?" Karin was really frightened now. It was two against one, and she had always been a little in awe of Darcy's hotshot husband. He wasn't the one she had wanted to hurt really. It was Darcy. It had always been about Darcy and her twin sister, Danielle. They had foiled all her plans and then taken away the inheritance she was due from their father.

"Yes, Karin. I'm here too," Mark announced boldly as he stepped around the corner from the other aisle. "I want you to tell us the truth about hiring some bogus employee to accuse me of faking and exaggerating stories and then pretending to be a witness and signing a false deposition. This is your last chance. Otherwise, you can spend all day being questioned by the police."

"What will happen to me if I confess?" Karin simpered. Her brave facade was slipping, and her voice shook as badly as her body.

"I won't do anything to you. I just want to tape your confession and play it for the people at the network to clear my name and restore my reputation with them. Then you'll be free to go on with your miserable life as long as you stay the hell away from me and my family."

"Can I have a drink?" Karin begged. She was unraveling fast and didn't know what to do. She wished Brett was with her. He'd be able to figure a way out of this. He was always so clever. Why had she left him back at the flophouse?

"No, your confession first." Mark was adamant. "Then the drink."

"Okay, damn it," Karin barely whispered and seemed to crumple into a ball on the floor. "It went down just as you said. When I told Sonny I wanted to get you and Darcy fired, he agreed to help in return for a few sexual favors. He had a friend who worked for ESPN, and he persuaded her to make up the bogus charges against you.

"Brett and I claimed to have been standing outside your office door and overheard you on the phone. We said you were discussing making up a baseball story to boost your program's rating. It was a damn good plan, and it worked," she said triumphantly, proud of what she'd done. "We thought ESPN would pay us a lot of money to keep quiet and to keep the story out of the papers. But they only gave us a few thousand and made us sign papers that we would never tell what had happened, or we'd go to jail."

Mark took out his tape recorder and shoved it near Karin's moth. "Keep talking."

Karin admitted to framing Mark and implicating Sonny Kasem and Brett too. Mark again assured her that he wouldn't initiate any charges. He only wanted to clear his name. Revenge wasn't normally his thing, although because of his deep love for Darcy and Danielle, he was enjoying seeing Karin squirm. When Karin finished her confession, Darcy marched up to the cashier, bought a bottle of cheap vodka, and handed it to her stepmother.

"This wasn't the only time you made false charges against someone, I'd bet. It's a pattern with you and Brett. Every time you get down and out, you pull a scam that hurts other people and lines your filthy pockets with tainted money."

Karen refused to look at Mark but made no denial.

"Maybe you should consider going to AA," Darcy said seriously. "You could get sober and maybe make a decent future for yourself."

"La de da." Karin sneered as she twisted off the cap of the bottle and took a long gulp of the fiery liquid. "Always a Pollyanna, aren't you?" She clutched the vodka snugly to her chest and walked unsteadily out of the store. Turning back to face Darcy and Mark, she screamed, "Kiss my ass!" and gave them the finger.

CHAPTER 68

Danielle

Danielle and Don waited for Darcy and Mark. She had dressed Caroline and Freddy in matching outfits, hoping to take some family pictures. If they came out well, she planned to use one of them for her holiday cards. Freddy was already fidgeting and tugging at his bow tie when his aunt and uncle walked in.

"My, don't you look handsome." Darcy kissed her nephew. "Where's your little sister?"

Caroline skipped into the living room, wearing an adorable navy-and-white sailor suit with matching navy ballet slippers. She ran to Mark and snuggled into his arms.

Danielle asked Don to take some family photos. Finally, he got what Danielle considered a good shot, where everyone was smiling, and no one's eyes were closed or crossed. Happy with the results, she guided everyone to the living room. Don served drinks.

"Don and I had the most exciting day," Danielle said proudly, "and in more ways than one. We came up with an addition to our Healing Words and Healing Hands programs. We're going to start a foundation and combine the other two programs into it. Don's agreed to be the co-CEO. We haven't come up with a name yet, but we're working on it."

"That's wonderful news." Darcy beamed. She was so proud of her sister's selfless endeavors. Danielle had turned her writing talents into something that helped suffering people, and she did it so humbly. "Tell us about it."

Danielle and Don explained that they were going to apply the principles of their two existing programs to include bereavement counseling. Then Danielle sheepishly admitted that she had written a book about her own journey through grief and had sent it in July to a few literary agents to test the waters. "I'm hopeful that some publisher will take it on. If it's any good, it can also be used as additional material for this new program."

Mark and Darcy were intrigued and wholeheartedly offered their congratulations.

"You two have been very busy," Mark joked. He had always been impressed with Don's managerial skills and Danielle's foresight.

"More than you know," Don said with a sly smile. "Danielle and I have more news."

"Oh?" Darcy looked at them with curiosity. They were glowing.

"Yes." Danielle smiled happily. "Don and I have decided that we've been immersed in our own personal grief long enough, and we're ready to move forward … to put the joy of living back into our lives."

"What exactly does that mean?" Mark asked with curiosity.

"It means we've decided to move in together and become partners in life as well as partners in business." Don beamed as he took Danielle's hand and kissed it gallantly. "I'm here so much anyway that we thought it would be more convenient if I moved in. I know that doesn't sound too romantic, but it's our love story. We'll be a real family, and I will look out for and love Freddy and Caroline too. They need a father figure in their lives. I know I can't ever replace Alex and don't want to, but there's room in Danielle's heart for another love … and thankfully she's chosen me!"

"Oh my! That's wonderful," Darcy exclaimed. She had hoped for this outcome. "I'm so happy for you both."

"This is great news, Buddy." Mark slapped Don affectionately on his back. "Welcome to this wacky family."

"We're not getting married, at least not now … just living together." Danielle wanted to be sure her sister understood. "But Don makes me and the children so happy. We both believe this is the right next step."

"Whatever makes you happy," Darcy reassured her sister. "I'm a modern lady too, you know, so the two of you living together sans marriage doesn't shock me at all. Mark and I did it. As a matter of fact, I think it's kind of cute."

"To Danielle and Don." Mark raised his glass in a toast.

"Yes, to Danielle and Don," Darcy concurred, clinking her glass with the others. "And by the way, Mark and I have some important news of our own."

Danielle looked at her sister expectantly.

"This afternoon we tracked down and confronted Karin about being responsible for the ESPN fiasco. We followed her to a seedy liquor store on the Bowery. Then we got her to confess to making up the charges and falsifying the evidence. She did it for money naturally. We have it all on tape. It'll explain everything in more detail later. This is your night, and we won't let stepmother dearest ruin it. But as an aside, Karin was actually so undone by seeing us that she peed in her pants."

"Not a pretty site." Mark laughed.

CHAPTER 69

Darcy

Darcy and Mark took Karin's confession tape to Bill Robinson. They handed it to the lawyer, who promised to handle the ESPN situation for them. They were going back to DC later that afternoon.

Mark didn't care about a money settlement offered from the network; he was rich enough. Instead, he demanded a public apology, which stated that he was innocent of any wrongdoing and had been maliciously maligned and set up by vindictive people in an effort to extort money from ESPN.

Mr. Robinson shook Mark's hand. "I'm glad we got to the bottom of what happened. And I'll get you your public apology and see that its published in the top-ten newspapers in the country and on every ESPN television and radio channel. Hopefully we all will have no more dealings with Karin. She's a lonely, defeated, bitter woman now and all because of her greedy, vicious acts. I bet Fred Coulter is in heaven laughing right now."

"I'm just glad it's over," Darcy said thoughtfully. "Do you think ESPN will try to prosecute her?"

"Yes. First, I think they will go after the woman who made the false allegations against Mark at Karin's direction and then against Karin and Brett. They can't be allowed to make fools of everyone like they did." Mr. Robinson was adamant. "I know Mark promised Karin he wouldn't charge her, but ESPN made no such proclamation. Karin will have her day in court. Mark my words."

"Thanks for everything." Darcy shook hands with the lawyer.

"Now it's time to get back to the business of helping Nathan run the country." Mark smiled. He was eager to get back to Washington.

They left the attorney's office and were back in their own offices a few hours later.

* * *

Darcy's phone rang the minute she walked into her DC condo that evening. It was Ginger Gardner. She wanted to tell Darcy everything the babies were doing and invite Darcy and Mark to come to dinner and spend some time with them.

"I'd love to see the boys," Darcy exclaimed happily. "Is everything going okay with them … and with you and Lloyd and Edward?"

"Yes, everything's good, and the two nannies are working out well. Edward has quite a little family to take care of, and he's loving every minute of it. We've made some changes in our living arrangements," Ginger said mysteriously. "I'd like to tell you about them. Can you come to dinner tomorrow night at seven? And try to be on time please, because the babies get their last feeding at eight, and then they're put to bed."

"Will do." Darcy smiled. Ginger never gave up her controlling ways.

* * *

The next evening Darcy and Mark pulled up to the Gardners' suburban mansion at 6:50. "Better early than late." Mark snickered.

George, the trusted family butler, opened the door and ushered them inside. "Everyone's in the living room," he announced proudly. He was happy to see Darcy again. She had always held a special place in his heart. He had known her since she was barely out of her teens and had been dating Jason. He studied her now and reflected that she had only grown more beautiful in the ensuing years. Marriage to Mr. Donavan had obviously agreed with her.

"Welcome, welcome." Lloyd rose to greet them. Ginger had one baby on her lap, and Edward carried the other.

"It's so good to have everyone here together," Edward said with a broad smile. "Life is full of such strange and wonderful surprises."

Darcy noticed Ginger had her gin and tonic close by. The fact that Thanksgiving was only a week away didn't prompt Ginger to give up her summer drink. She noticed Lloyd had switched to rum and Coke.

"What's the new living arrangements you mentioned on the phone?" Darcy asked as soon as she took Jackson from Edward and started to play with the four-month-old.

Ginger hugged baby Jason and grinned. "We are such an unconventional family now that we decided to take it to the next logical step."

Darcy and Mark waited for her to say more.

"Lloyd and I wanted the babies and Edward to all be under the same roof with us. It's much easier than driving the beltway every day to visit them. So we invited Edward to come live with us here. He put his place in Virginia on the market and moved in here last week."

"That's a great idea," Mark said. "It will certainly be easier on everyone."

"But how's that going to work?" Darcy was curious but didn't want to address the elephant in the room. Ginger knew exactly what she was asking.

"You're curious about the sleeping arrangements?" Ginger smiled slyly. "I don't blame you. This is what we've worked out. Lloyd will live in the guest house. That's his private place, and *no* one," she said, looking pointedly at Edward, "will be allowed in there except George when the place needs cleaning."

"I see." Darcy grinned. Edward had been put on notice that there was to be no hanky-panky between himself and Lloyd. She had to admire Ginger. She was a gutsy lady. This time the bargain with her husband had nothing to do with money.

"And," Ginger continued, "I've gotten too old to tackle the stairs. Even with our elevator, I feel safer on the ground floor. So I've moved downstairs to the first-floor master suite and given Edward my old rooms upstairs. Needless to say, we will redecorate them to suit Edward and the boys' needs. He and the twins will have the whole upper floor, and the two nannies will be just down the hall."

"It's a great arrangement." Edward smiled. "I couldn't be more thrilled. The boys will have this enormous yard to play in as they get older, and they'll always be somebody home, besides the nannies, to play with and love them. I can't thank Ginger and Lloyd enough."

"It is our pleasure." Ginger's eyes misted. "I think Jason would be very happy about our new arrangements."

The nannies appeared and whisked the babies off to bed after everyone had hugged and kissed them good night.

"Dinner is served," George announced. "But who shall I sit at the head and foot of the table?" he asked Ginger.

"Put Mark at the head and Darcy at the other end." She looked at Darcy and blew her a kiss. "It's time the new generation of our eclectic family took their rightful places. Whenever Mark and Darcy are here, they are every bit as much family as any one of us."

CHAPTER 70

Danielle

Danielle and Don were busy preparing Thanksgiving dinner for themselves and the children. Ray Smith was flying in from Boston to join them. Darcy and Mark had been invited, but they had decided to celebrate the festivities with Nathan and Connie and their family (Ginger, Lloyd, Edward, Jackson, and Jason). They were all going to Camp David for the weekend.

Don had recently found a tenant for his apartment and moved his clothing, favorite books, and some personal articles into Danielle's condo. He'd sold or had given away what he didn't need. Danielle had cleaned out a few closets and plenty of drawers, so Don had room for everything he'd brought and would feel at home.

Freddy and Caroline didn't fully understand what was happening but were thrilled that Dr. D was living with them now and would be around to give them piggyback rides or read them stories. They had agreed to call him "Daddy Don." It was more intimate than Dr. D. They were their own special family and were looking forward to spending their first holiday together as such.

Ray Smith was very happy for them. He was responsible for introducing Danielle and Don and was delighted that their work relationship had blossomed into a love match. He could see how good they were with each other and that the children were happy too. Freddy had been too young to remember Alex, and Caroline had never seen him.

Darcy told them their real daddy was in heaven, watching over them, but they were too young to understand the concept.

After a delicious turkey feast, Dr. Smith announced that he felt it was the right time for him to step down as chair of the board of directors. He knew Danielle and Don were starting a new foundation to encompass all their programs, Healing Words, Healing Hands, and Healing Hearts; and he felt they should select a new board and executive team going forward.

Don thanked him for his service and made a few suggestions from his pool of medical friends and associates. Ray also had some ideas of his own. Danielle was happy to leave the selection up to the two of them. She was already so busy with all her domestic responsibilities. Getting the new foundation up and running and financially solvent was her new mission. After they talked a bit more, she announced that she had some good news to share.

"I've been so busy that I forgot to tell you that last week I heard back from Ace Publishing, and they are willing to take on my book, *Living through Grief*. It will make a good textbook for our Healing Hearts concept, and I'm hopeful that it'll reach a mass audience through internet purchases."

"That's wonderful news." Dr. Smith beamed. "I knew you had it in you, Danielle." He got up from the table to give her an enormous bear hug. "Alex would be so proud of you," he whispered.

"I hope so," she whispered back. "I've waited all this time for some sign from him, but so far communications from heaven have been in silent mode."

"Sometimes no news is good news." He grinned. "I think you are my most interesting patient ever and certainly the most accomplished."

"I don't know about that." She was embarrassed. "But I owe so much to you, Ray, and you too, Don." She looked lovingly at the two men who had been so instrumental in her recovery from the loss of Alex and for the success she had made of her programs.

"This has been an interesting and rewarding year," she reflected. "And I have so much to be grateful for. She thought for a moment and said, "In no particular order, my despicable stepmother, Karin, has been indicted for perjury and fraud, and is in jail, awaiting trial. So, in her case, justice has finally been served.

"After hearing Karin's confession, ESPN publicly apologized to Darcy and Mark for their egregious mistake of firing Mark with no reliable evidence. The network has repeatedly tried to make financial restitution, but Darcy and Mark didn't want their money, just his reputation restored."

She looked around the table and continued. "Connie and Nathan have weathered political storms and survived scandalous personal gossip. They've come through it all stronger and more popular than ever.

"Thankfully, our country is in good hands. Darcy and Mark are thrilled to be living in DC. They love their jobs and are spending lots of time with Ginger and Jason's precious boys. Those babies seem to have brought out Darcy's maternal side. On this Thanksgiving Day, everyone I love seems to be in a happy and healthy place. God is good indeed. Wow, that was a long-winded speech." She shook off her embarrassment. She wasn't normally so sentimental.

"Yes," Don agreed wholeheartedly. "And I am thankful too. My heart is full. I have Danielle and the children in my life. I never thought after Rachelle and Carly died that I'd ever smile again, much less find love and a family life. Danielle and I are embarking on a new adventure with this foundation. I can't wait to get to the office every morning to face the challenges and then come home at night to be with my new family. This has been a wonderful Thanksgiving and the first of many, many more." He blew Danielle a kiss. "Where's the pumpkin pie?"

"Where do you think?" She grinned mysteriously. "Freddy, please show Daddy Don where the dessert is."

Freddy proudly stood up from the table and walked over to Hippocrates. "Hipp's got it." He giggled. The statue was holding the pie on his silver tray. It was only fitting. After all, he was part of the family too.

"Happy Thanksgiving, everyone," Danielle said.

"To you too," Dr. Smith echoed. "And thank you for including me in this wonderful occasion. By the way"—he turned to look at them both—"have you come up with a name for your foundation?"

"Yes," Don and Danielle said in unison. "The Alex Stone Foundation."

CHAPTER 71

Darcy

Darcy and Mark held hands as they walked around the beautiful grounds of Camp David. The rustic presidential retreat was located in the wooded hills of Catoctin Mountain Park in Maryland, a thirty-minute helicopter ride from the White House. The president and his immediate family (their son, Frank, and his wife, Amy) were staying in the largest cabin, Aspen Lodge, which was surrounded by twelve additional guest cabins. The main house featured a heated swimming pool, a hot tub, and one golf hole with multiple tees. Various activities were planned for the weekend, climaxed by a pitch-and-putt contest at the golf hole on the last day.

Darcy and Mark had been assigned to one of the beautiful guest cabins, as had Lloyd and Ginger Gardner. Edward and his twins had another. The nannies had been given the holiday weekend off because there were so may adults willing to help look after the boys. It was to be a true old-fashioned family Thanksgiving at one of the world's most famous locations.

"What a beautiful place," Darcy said, in awe of her surroundings. Even though the fall foliage was over and the tree limbs were mostly bare, the grounds and mountains in the background were gorgeous and peaceful. Steam was rising off the heated swimming pool and outdoor jacuzzi. As they continued their morning walk, Mark waved to Connie and Nathan, who were sitting in the hot tub, relaxing.

"Can you believe everything that's happened this year?" Mark said thoughtfully.

"We did have some adventures and some laughs," Darcy agreed. "I can still see the reporters' stunned faces when they realized Danielle and I had tricked them with the tapes of us going in and out of the Oval with Nathan. That was pretty priceless. It felt like old times."

"And what about when you switched places on the set of *Real People?* To this day, William Bell doesn't have a clue." Mark laughed. "You two really pulled that switch off, and the program is now in contention for an Emmy."

"I know, and by us switching places, it brought Don and Danielle together. When Don thought Danielle was romantically interested in William, it made him realize how much he cared for her. I'm sorry we're not with them and the kids this Thanksgiving, but giving them their own family space is important. There will be many more holidays for us to share together."

"Not to change the subject, but I wonder what Karin will be having for dinner today. I doubt prison food is very tasty." Mark made a disgusted face.

"It's what she deserves," Darcy said stiffly. "I'm trying hard to forgive her, but it's really difficult. If she'd shown some remorse, it would be easier. One thing I know for sure is that she won't be washing the meal down with her favorite vodka."

Mark laughed. "Don't be too sure. She's pretty cagey, and I wouldn't put sleeping with a guard or even with the warden past her. She'd do it in a heartbeat if the reward was booze."

Darcy grinned. "You may be right. She's so damn entitled. I don't believe she'll ever accept that the world doesn't owe her everything. Maybe this jail time will be a dose of reality. Maybe she'll sober up for good."

Before they could continue the discussion, Edward came by, pushing a double stroller. The twins were bundled up inside with little matching snowsuits, mittens, and caps with their names on them. It had been Ginger's fall project to knit them for her grandsons.

"Hi, you two lovebirds," Edward called out but kept on walking. "As you can see, the boys are benefiting from my exercising. I bought one of those newfangled watches that counts my steps. I'm trying for ten thousand a day. It's exhausting."

"But it's so good for you." Mark laughed. "I should get one of those things myself."

"Well, personally I'm glad this year is almost over," Darcy said. "I never want to go through a health scare like I had ever again. I'm so grateful for my wonderful doctor and to you for your support."

Mark kissed her softly. "I was so worried about you too," he admitted. "No more medical issues. Promise?"

"Yes, I promise." She smiled at her wonderful husband. "I've been wanting to ask you something. Are you really satisfied with ESPN's apology and their mea culpas? Have you truly put the whole terrible incident behind you, or do you secretly want to return to broadcasting once we're done here at the White House?"

"Why do you ask?" He looked at her curiously. "I thought we agreed it was over and done with and that we'd never work for ESPN in any capacity again, even though they do keep making tantalizing overtures."

"Because I have a confession to make."

"Oh?" He regarded her with curiosity.

"Right when you were fired, the same day actually, I had planned to tell you that I was tired of covering and dissecting sports … that I thought there was something more meaningful and important that we could do with our lives. Then boom. Out of nowhere, the false charges arose, and we got fired. Believe me, that was never the way I wanted *Speaking of Sports with Donavan & Donavan* to end. However, since the minute it happened, I've felt guilty, like it was some kind of karma … the universe saying to me, 'Be careful what you wish for. Now see what you've done.'"

"That's silly, darling. You are not to blame in any way, but thanks for telling me. I wish I'd known you were unhappy. I would have made any change you wanted. I hope you know that. We're a team, no matter what." He took her face in his hands and tenderly kissed her again. "If we hadn't lost our jobs, I doubt we would have accepted Nathan and

Connie's offer to come to DC, and look how life changing that experience has been. Talk about doing something important ... we're really doing it."

"You're so right. But have you ever wondered if it was a coincidence that Nathan called us exactly when he did, or whether a little birdie hinted to him that we might leap at the chance for a new start?"

She had always been suspicious about the timing of the job offers. "I don't know for sure, but I've always suspected Danielle had something to do with it. She wasn't too surprised when we said we were moving to DC, only with the suddenness of it. But if she was responsible in any way, I sincerely thank her."

"I suppose we could simply ask her. But what difference does it really make? We are so happy here. She's ecstatic in New York with Don, and Connie and Nathan are thrilled to be in the White House. We all have so much to be grateful for."

"Yes, we do." Mark smiled. "Brr, it's getting chilly. Let's go inside. I think there's a turkey in the kitchen that's calling our names and two precious little boys who are waiting for us. Happy Thanksgiving, my love."

"Happy Thanksgiving to you too and to the whole world." She whirled around with glee and dragged him toward the Aspen Lodge, where their miraculously unique family was waiting to share the holiday meal with them.

EPILOGUE

Two years later

On Danielle and Don's wedding day, it was raining heavily. Danielle finally got the signal from Alex that she had yearned for. The New York City sky was gray and overcast, but just as Danielle began to recite her vows, the rain stopped, and the radiant sun broke through the clouds. A magnificent double rainbow appeared over Manhattan. Danielle looked at the church window and sent a silent thank-you to her beloved Alex. She knew he had given her permission to remarry.

* * *

Danielle and Don were in their designated chairs on the podium. Freddy and Caroline were dressed in their Sunday finest and squirming restlessly in the seats beside them. They had left the newest addition of their family at home in New York City with their nanny, Lynn. The two-month-old baby sister, Alexis, was too young to travel to DC in the cold January weather.

In a row behind them, Edward, Ginger, Lloyd, and the twin boys were happily ensconced and waiting for the festivities to begin. Ginger was judiciously passing out candy to keep the boys sitting quietly in their places.

Darcy and Mark sat in the first row. Darcy looked beautiful in her inaugural outfit, but the spectacular St. John's form-fitting navy wool coat and matching suede high-heeled boots she'd worn the last time on this podium had been left at home in her closet. Seven months pregnant with twins, she was content to wear loose-fitting clothing and comfortable shoes for the time being.

The strains of "Hail to the Chief" began as Connie and Nathan Pierce, followed by the vice president and her husband, slowly began walking down the stairs, greeting family and friends on both sides. The atmosphere was congenial and celebratory.

After an arduous campaign, the Pierces' presidential ticket had won an overwhelming victory at the polls. So at precisely twelve o'clock noon, Nathan stood with his hand on the Bible and took the oath of office for the second time. His wife, the First Lady, stood proudly by his side. Darcy and Danielle were both there too.

No switch was necessary this time. The indomitable Coulter twins had once again prevailed.